ADULT
WORLD

Christopher Scott Grimaldi

PELORUS PRESS

PELORUS PRESS

Published by Pelorus Press
12363 Academy Road, Philadelphia, PA 19154

PUBLISHER'S NOTE
This is a work of fiction. Names, characters, places, and incidents
either are the product of the author's imagination or are used
fictitiously, and any resemblance to actual persons, living or dead,
business establishments, events, or locales is entirely coincidental.

ISBN 978-0615600802

Cover art by Scott Pehnke
"Man/Woman/Earth" symbol logo © Christopher Scott Grimaldi

Printed in the United States of America

For her

FIRST

Sometimes life throws you wicked curveballs. In the second half of my senior year in high school, just when I think I have the world figured out, it hurls a couple of doozies. I never even see them coming.

Or maybe I do … but, like a fool, I choose to ignore them and hope they don't take my head off.

It all starts simple enough on my birthday. I wake for school like I do every morning, only this time right at the end of a sex dream.

If you're a guy, you know how these dreams usually end. If you're a girl … well, let's just say that I need to rinse the front of my underwear in the bathroom sink.

Of course, I then have to hang it on the edge of the trash can in my room to dry so my mom won't see it and I can avoid any embarrassment.

I know; it's gross. But most things that involve sex kind of are, aren't they?

So begins the eighteenth year of my life.

Once my underwear situation's taken care of, I take my morning shower and eat a couple bowls of sugar-coated kids' cereal, like I usually do. The only difference in my ritual is that today my mom's left a birthday card on the table in front of me. "BRIAN," it says in big letters on the baby blue envelope - as if it could be for anyone else.

I know what's inside - other than the greeting card, that is: a hundred dollar bill. Working two jobs and all, she doesn't have much time to shop for birthday gifts. So she gives me cash, which is fine by me. I can always use it.

Most days my mom's gone by the time I wake up, but today I think she's stayed to wish me a happy birthday. When she walks into the kitchen, all dressed up in her work blazer and slacks, her hair tied up to look more office professional, I lift the envelope and say, "Thanks."

She nods. "You're welcome."

We don't kiss or hug or anything corny like that. We've never done the whole PDA thing - y'know, Public Displays of Affection. At least she hasn't. So I haven't, either.

I think she gets that from my grandparents - her parents, the Fitzgeralds; not my dad's, the Hartmans. But we haven't talked to that side of the family since my dad died, so there's no way I could know for sure.

"You're not going to open your card?" she says, looking disappointed.

So I do. And inside there are *two* hundred dollar bills this time.

"Mom ... it's too much."

"No, it's not. I wish it could be more. You'll need it next year."

I will, too. College isn't going to be cheap, especially where I'm going - or where I want to go, I should say ... if I can afford it. The University of the Arts. In Philadelphia. It's a forty-five minute drive from where I live in Pennsylvania - just far enough from home for me to be on my own, but close enough to check in on my mom when I need to. If I didn't, I don't know who would. It's not like she has a steady boyfriend or anything. She's been seeing a lot of this guy Gary lately, but I'm sure it'll end soon, like all the others.

She's never seemed all that interested in dating. Well, she's dated a little; it's a full-on relationship I don't think she's interested in. I'm not sure why.

"Okay, I'm off," she says after filling her travel mug with coffee. "You're home for dinner, right?" I shrug. "C'mon. You only turn eighteen once."

"You only turn every age once."

"I know some women who've been turning twenty-nine for years," she says with a wink and stares at me until I relent.

"All right. Yeah, I'll be here for dinner."

"Good." She heads toward the door, stops, stares at me, and smiles. "Happy Birthday."

I smile back. "Thanks, Mom."

She stares another few seconds, as if there's something else she wants to say, but leaves without saying it.

When I hear the front door close, I return to my breakfast, shovel in a few spoonfuls of my magically delicious cereal, and examine my card. On the front is a bright, multi-colored "HAPPY BIRTHDAY" that looks like it's made of Play-Doh or something.

It's strange because it seems like a card made for a child, but it can't be, since there's also a big "18" below it in the same lettering, only larger. I guess it's kind of fitting, though.

Happy Birthday to me.

As long as I can remember, my best friend in the world has been Mike Welch. He was born a couple months after I was and has always lived three houses down, so all throughout our childhood we went fishing or rode bikes or played baseball together almost every day. Sometimes we even just hung out and talked about stuff. We sort of became like brothers, which was nice - especially since neither of us had one of our own.

Like most mornings, on my birthday I walk to Mike's house to hitch a ride to North Penn High School. It's either that or take the bus - and riding shotgun with Mike in the BMW his dad bought him sure beats dealing with a bunch of rowdy kids trapped in a ratty, yellow school bus.

We leave early on Fridays because Mike swings by his dad's business, Adult World, to get his allowance.

If the name doesn't give it away, Adult World is a porn store. It's been around for like thirty years or something, but Mr. Welch has only owned it for the last ten or so.

You can apparently purchase all sorts of X-rated items there. I say "apparently" because I've never been inside and don't know exactly what's there. I've only seen it from the outside, while Mike runs in to get his money, because I've never been old enough to enter.

I suppose it wouldn't have been a big deal to sneak a peek, but Mike's dad is kind of firm about the "under eighteen years old" restriction. Mike's only an exception because he's the boss's son. And even then, Mr. Welch doesn't like him to be there very long, in case some police officer or town official tries to get him for "corrupting the morals of a minor" - or whatever.

Of course, now that I'm eighteen and technically an adult, I can go in. So after Mike parks and gets out of the car, he eggs me on to follow him. "C'mon. You're old enough now."

Still, I don't think I'm quite ready to see what's inside, which is probably the real reason I didn't go in before. I figure some things are probably better left a mystery for now. "That's okay. I'll pass."

"Oh, don't be such a puss," Mike says.

His peer pressure makes me consider following him in and I glance at the store while I decide. It's strange how it resembles a typical, suburban brick ranch house, only painted a dull gray. And I mean, *all* of it's painted gray - even the boards placed over the windows. The shingles on the roof are the same shade, so that the whole thing looks like a square rain cloud fallen to the ground.

The sign on the roof reads the name of the store in an out-of-date font with rounded letters. The *A* looks sort of like a penis, the *W* a pair of breasts. Below it, in normal black letters, it says, "For Everything In-Store."

"Bro, this is the way of the world," Mike lectures me. "The sooner you face it, the better off you'll be." He closes his car door and heads toward the store, clearly assuming I'll follow.

I look around to make sure there's no one who could see me and decide, *Eh, what the hell. I* am *old enough. I should be able to handle whatever I see. Hell, I've probably seen it all before, anyway.*

Right?

I shrug, take a deep breath, and follow Mike.

The inside of the store, if it was once a house, no longer looks like one in any way that I can see. It's divided into two main sections, with the register on a raised platform that overlooks and separates the two.

As I enter I can see that on one side, to the left, there's merchandise, videos, that kind of thing. On the other side, to the right, is a dark area with rows of what look like those photo booths you see in arcades - only instead of curtains to hide the people inside, there are public restroom-style stall doors. To add to the bathroom effect, I can see men's feet below the doors of some of the booths. Judging from the flickering light and the occasional sound of voices - some talking, some squealing with what sounds like pleasure - and bad music, I can tell they're watching sex videos.

I remember Mike mentioning the booths, but I guess I never put two and two together - or if I did, maybe I blocked it out. And at first I don't think too much of it ... that is, until I remember what it is people usually do when they watch porn videos.

"Is that ... ? Are they actually ... ?" I ask Mike. He nods and laughs when he sees the disgusted look on my face. It's kind of hard to believe anybody would do that in a public place, even behind a closed stall door. Horrifying, actually. But they do. And there's the proof.

I try to put it out of my mind as we approach the cash register.

"Hey Tommy," Mike says to a skinny, unshaven man in his late twenties, maybe early thirties, who sits behind the counter. He looks bored - really bored.

Tommy barely nods back a greeting. I'm not sure if he

doesn't like Mike or just doesn't care about his presence … or is just jaded in general. "He around?"

"On his way …" Tommy says, then looks at me. "He allowed in here? You know how pissed he gets - unless he's gonna spend money. You gonna spend money?"

I shrug. I have no intention of spending any money, but figure it's safer not to answer one way or the other.

"Oh, don't worry," Mike says. "He's eighteen."

Tommy squints at me. "You sure? He doesn't look it."

I nod in agreement as Mike says, "Yeah."

Tommy shrugs okay and goes back to work - although he's not really doing anything at the moment. Still, he seems bothered by Mike's attempts to engage him in small talk and shrugs each time Mike asks how business has been - if it's been busy, if there've been a lot of sales, stuff like that. I don't see how it's any of Mike's business, but I guess at one point, when he's old enough to work here or maybe eventually take over, it will be.

I decide to tune them both out and take a couple minutes to survey the merchandise area now that I have the official all-clear to be here.

I must say, I'm completely thrown by what I see.

Of course, there are shelves and shelves of videos with crude photos of naked men and women - mostly women - all over them; that I expected. What I didn't expect was the wide variety of bizarre non-video items. There are vibrators and blowup dolls, which you'd expect, but there are also a lot of other things … strange things: rubber masturbators in mouth and vagina shapes, electric cock rings, English cock and ball cages, anal speculums, and vibrating anal plugs, to name a few.

Even after the years of Mike talking about the store since his dad bought it, I've never heard of half the stuff - let alone guessed what most of it's for. But there they all are, out in the open, for sale, like it's normal. And it is, I guess … at least in Adult World.

I'm so blown away by what I see that I nearly trip over a chubby employee stocking videos. "Sorry," I say.

"No problem," he responds with a slight smile. He can no doubt read the shock - horror, even - on my face.

At that moment, Mr. Welch walks through the front door, looks around, and heads straight for the two of us. He seems to be angry and at first I fear he's coming right at me, maybe because I'm in here and he thinks I'm too young to be.

Before he gets to me, though, Mike calls to him. He stops and turns to see him. "Yeah. I'll be right with you."

Mr. Welch turns back and only then seems to notice that it's me in the store. "Brian? Hey. What're you doing in here?"

"It's okay, Dad. He turned eighteen today."

Mr. Welch's face softens. "Really?" he says, then smiles. "Heh. How 'bout that. Look at you, all grown up." He rubs my head and messes my hair. "Seems like only yesterday they brought you home from the hospital."

I smile. It's strange to think that I've known him all my life. In fact, because of Mike, I probably spent more time with him than any other adult besides my mom - especially after my dad died. He even taught me how to hold a bat and catch a baseball when he coached Mike and me in Little League, which was nice; he didn't have to do that.

He's the closest thing I had to a father when I was little. But I haven't seen him much in the past few years, not since he moved out of the house on my street - where Mike and his mom, the former Mrs. Welch, still live.

"How's your mother, anyway?" Mr. Welch says.

"Good. Busy as ever."

"Terrific. Fantastic woman, your mom. Really fantastic." He nods as the employee who was near me stands and heads toward the register. His movement draws Mr. Welch's attention. His eyes follow the employee, then he glances back at me, says, "Excuse me," and walks after him. "What happened Wednesday night?" I hear him whisper.

The employee doesn't seem to know what he's talking about. "What?"

Mr. Welch leads him behind the register and through a door to the back room of the store. It seems like something strange is going on and I wonder what it might be until Mike waves a large, black, rubber penis in my face.

"Here ya go," he says. "For Jenny."

"Jenny" is Jennifer Kinney, the girl I've been seeing for a couple weeks now. I haven't even gotten to second base with her yet, so I certainly can't use a sex toy like that. I doubt I'll ever get to *that* point with her, anyway.

I grab Mike's arm and shove it away, which is my normal reaction to anybody waving anything in my face, let alone a huge rubber dick. I push it back in his face and I guess I grab him harder than I expected because he makes a face and says, "Damn, Bro. You been working out …"

It's true; I have been working out. I bought a cheap weight set and lift a few times a week. It's definitely made me stronger.

"Or maybe it's all that …" Mike makes a palm-up fist and jerks it toward and away from his crotch.

I groan at the joke.

"When you gonna stop bein' a bat boy with that girl, anyway?" he says.

I don't answer. There's no point. It only encourages him.

"You must be hornier than a marching band on Ecstasy."

"A what?" I say.

"You heard me."

I laugh - and continue to in the hope that it'll make him forget his original question. But it doesn't work.

"Seriously," he says. "How long's it been since you got any, anyway? Two years?"

"I've done all right." I've actually dated a few girls and gotten pretty far. I had my fingers in a few of them, they got me off with their hand, that kind of thing. Not all the way, but I was clearly rounding second and heading for third, which isn't bad, considering how little effort I've always put into base-running.

"That other shit ain't sex," Mike says.

"Oh, like you're swimming in it."

"I hold my own."

"Two, three times a day, I'm sure," I say.

"Boys will be boys ..." he says and flicks his eyebrows up and down. "Sometimes you just gotta bunt ... but look who I'm telling." He laughs at me as his dad returns from the back with the employee who's no longer wearing his staff shirt. He's now carrying his coat and a duffel bag as Mr. Welch leads him toward the front door.

"What about the money you owe me?" he says to Mr. Welch, who continues to usher him out of the store.

"Tell ya what, I'll deduct what you owe *me* and mail the check to you. You should be happy you're getting anything."

Mr. Welch closes the door behind the now apparent *ex*-employee and turns back to Tommy. "You believe that? After all I did for him?"

Tommy shrugs. "We coulda used him tomorrow, Boss."

Mr. Welch makes a face. "Oh. Right. Well, who do I have to take his place?"

"You already got everybody scheduled. And I'm sure Charlie'll come in - not that he's worth that much, especially once *she* shows up." Tommy tilts his head toward a poster of a beautiful woman's face. Below the poster is the caption, "Meet Rita Hanson. Saturday, February 26th." Tomorrow's the twenty-sixth.

Mr. Welch sighs, thinks a second, then looks at me and smiles. I'm not sure why at first. He moves closer and puts his arm around my shoulder. "Brian, my boy ..."

I quickly realize that he wants me to work for him. "Sorry," I say, "I, uh, already have to work tomorrow ... at Truman's." Truman's is the grocery store where I've worked since I was sixteen. It's a pretty good job, as jobs go. It beats scrubbing pots in a hot kitchen, which is what I did before I turned sixteen and could apply to Truman's. Plus, they pay more than minimum wage.

"So?" Mr. Welch says. "Call in sick. I'll make it worth your while."

I scrunch my face with doubt. I don't want to lie to my boss at Truman's. I don't like to lie at all, in fact. And, frankly, I'm not sure I want to work in this place, with the booths in the back and the weird sexual things and all that.

Mr. Welch looks disappointed. He takes his arm off my shoulder and stares at me. "What time do you have to go in?"

"Um, four."

"Perfect," he says and holds his hands out to show me the problem's solved. "I'll only need you for a few hours. Eleven to three or so."

I'm still doubtful.

"How's ten bucks an hour sound?" he adds. "Cash."

It sounds pretty good.

"Plus an extra ten. That's fifty bucks." He says it like it's a fortune ... and it is a lot of money compared to what I make at Truman's, especially since there won't be any taxes taken out.

I look at Mike, who has this weird look on his face. I wonder if he's jealous or something. It might bother him if I work for his dad.

I search for some kind of sign on his face to show me he's okay with it.

"Don't look at him," Mr. Welch says. "You can answer for yourself. You're a man now."

As I continue to think about it, Mr. Welch wears me down with a stare. I hate to let him down. I hate to disappoint anyone ... especially an adult. And it's only for a day, so ...

"Um, well, I guess I can -" I say.

"There ya go, Tommy," Mr. Welch says. "Problem solved."

Tommy nods. I don't think he cares either way.

Mr. Welch starts to walk away, but Mike stops him. "Uh, Dad ..."

"Oh, right." Mr. Welch opens the register and hands some money to Mike. As he does, he seems to make sure I see it, then says, "Brian, my boy, see you tomorrow, eleven sharp."

I nod.

"And happy birthday." He winks and continues through the door to the back of the store.

And just like that I have another job - if only for a day.

We still have some time to kill before school, so Mike and I go to North Penn's baseball field, where Mike likes to sit in the dugout and smoke his last full cigarette of the school day. He'll probably smoke at least three more in puffs here and there before the end of school, but that's beside the point.

Mike's funny that way; if there's a vice out there, he's only too happy to partake in it. And not halfway; he dives right in.

Like sex. If, based on my dream, it looks like *I* have sex on my mind, that's nothing compared to Mike. I might only think about it or dream about it, but he actually does it - or so he says. I think it's more important to him than just about anything.

Even while we're sitting there he's paging through an amateur pornography magazine he picked up from the out-of-date stack at Adult World.

"Ya gotta love this stuff," he says, turning the magazine this way and that as he looks at the images.

"Um, no ... I don't."

"No, seriously. It's amazing. Guys sending in pictures of their girlfriends, wives, whatever ..." He laughs and pushes the magazine in my face. "Look at this broad." It's funny the way he says words like "broad." Like he's fifty or something.

He points to a photo of this bleach-blonde woman spread eagle on a cheap mattress, using her fingertips to help the photographer get a better view. It's kind of gross - and frankly a little too crude to be sexy. Well, to me, anyway. I'm sure a lot of guys go for that - and maybe I should, or will one day. But right now I'm more into beauty. Like, I look at the woman's face, the angle of her body, more than anything. How would I change the image to make it look better, more beautiful? I know ... weird, right?

Mike's not like me, though. He totally gets turned on by the graphic, in-your-face stuff, like this woman on the bed. The more graphic, the better. But if I grew up the way he did, with his dad and the porn business and all, I'd probably be the same way.

"These people crack me up," he says.

I glance at the photo and fake like I'm impressed so he won't bother me about it anymore.

"'Look honey, we made it into *Beaver Hunt*,'" he says and laughs. "Probly shows this to his buddies, maybe frames it. So proud ..." He shakes his head, pages through a few more photos, then stops. "Hey, speakin' a beaver hunt, I put the deposit down on the shore place for Senior Week. I'm gonna need that three-hundred beans, plus another three when we go down."

"Aw, man, I don't know ..." I say. It's a lot of money - to me, anyway.

He stares. "Bro, you better not puss out. It's *Senior Week*. You *gotta* go."

Here on the east coast, or at least in Pennsylvania - and I guess New Jersey, too - almost everybody who graduates from high school goes down to the Jersey Shore for the week after graduation. Thus, "Senior Week" - although technically it should be called "Graduate Week."

Most people go to places like Wildwood or Sea Isle City because, from what I hear, those are the biggest party towns and the cops are more forgiving of the shenanigans kids get into - especially kids with their first taste of freedom. So there's a lot of drinking, sex, and who knows what else.

Mike wants to go to Wildwood, the name of which couldn't be more perfect for kids trying to get laid. He's talked about it for months. He can hardly wait.

I told him I'd go, but really I don't think I can afford it - and even if I could, I'm not sure I want to spend my money that way. So I tell Mike I don't think I'll be able to dip into my college fund to swing it.

"Dude, you gotta stop stressin' so much about money."

Of course he would say that. He's never had to worry about money in his life. He has it. Well, his dad does - and I suppose his mom does, too, ever since the divorce from Mr. Welch when Mike was a kid.

"Who's paying for your college?" I ask him.

He rolls his eyes. He knows what I mean.

"Just take a girl with you," I say.

"Bro, you don't bring sand to the beach."

"The Jersey Shore's been eroding for years. Even *they're* bringing sand to the beach these days."

"Yeah, whatever, Smart Guy," he says and tosses his cigarette on the ground. "You're comin' with me - even if I have to give you the dough, myself. I'll hire ya as my wing man or something."

I laugh as I stamp out the cigarette, pick the butt up, and put it in the trash can before we head to school for the day.

As Mike and I walk the hallways before homeroom, he's still trying to talk me into Senior Week. "I'm tellin' ya, you're gonna want that last crack at these girls before you're stuck at art school with all those dyke-y broads," he says. "Probly don't even shave their armpits ... to say nothing of what's down south. Yeesh!"

I can't help laughing whenever he says something like that. *I* would never do it, of course. I might occasionally *think* it, but I'd never say it. Mike does. And it cracks me up every time.

I don't laugh in front of Jennifer, though. I don't want her to believe I think it's funny or even remotely acceptable, especially with how things have been going for the past couple of weeks since we started dating.

I know that's not a lot of time, but the time we've had has been good. I kinda knew her before then, too. Last semester we had sixth period classes near each other and I saw her in the hallway almost every day.

I can't say it was love at first sight, because I'm not sure what that is, but I definitely saw something in her ... something I still see ... something beyond the blonde hair, blue eyes, and hard but flexible cheerleader body. I'm not sure what that "something" is, but it was, and is, enough to make me want to know her better.

She says she felt the same way about me from the start and now, after a few dates and a couple long, deep conversations - along with a little kissing - I guess we could be called boyfriend and girlfriend, even though we've never actually said it.

"Easy, Mikey," I say so he'll tone down the sex talk as we approach Jennifer at her locker, where I meet her every morning. Today, as if just for my birthday, she's as adorable as ever in her cheerleader uniform, which she's required to wear on game days.

Although I couldn't care less about some stupid basketball game or wrestling match, I'm always glad for them, if only to see the short skirt and tight, sleeveless jersey she and all the other girls on the squad wear.

She smiles when she sees me and we kiss hello, as usual. It's only a peck, though. I wish it could be more, but I'm just getting used to PDA's at this point.

"Hey, Jenny," Mike says.

She nods kind of a cold hello back to him.

"Awright, I'm outta here," he says. "Remember, Bro, don't make plans for tonight. We gotta celebrate."

Ever since we were kids, Mike and I have spent each other's birthdays together. It's a pretty cool tradition. So far we haven't missed one.

"Not sure where it's gonna be, though. I'll let ya know." He starts to walk away, then stops and turns. "Oh, and don't forget your skin mag." He tosses his copy of *Beaver Hunt* at me.

Great. This is just what Jennifer needs to see.

I let the magazine fall to the ground like it's plutonium or something and say, "That's not mine."

Mike laughs and continues on.

"Seriously," I say to Jennifer.

But she doesn't seem to care. I think - I hope - she knows it's not mine. Still, she has a hurt look on her face.

"What's the matter?"

"Nothing," she says. "It's okay. I just ... I didn't know you were going out with Mike tonight."

"Oh, well, yeah, we kinda always hang out together on our birthdays. It's kind of a *thing*."

She nods.

"I figured you probably didn't want to hang out with him and -" The school bell rings to call everybody to homeroom as I backpedal. "I mean, I figured we were going out tomorrow ... but if you want to come out tonight ... I'd like that. Really. I just thought -"

"That's okay. I don't want you to feel obligated,"

Jennifer says as she gathers the last of her books and closes her locker without looking at me. She appears to be okay, but I can tell she's not. "I can just see you tomorrow ... maybe."

Uh-oh.

I think I'm in trouble. "Will I see you after school?"

She shrugs.

I'm definitely in trouble. I get confirmation when I move in for a kiss and she's already walking away.

It may not seem like a big deal, but I feel terrible. I'm not sure why. I just do.

I normally don't think too much about stuff like this, but with her it's different. I really like her. I mean *really* like her. I wish I could explain why, but I can't totally. She just makes me feel better when I'm with her - less awkward or something. I feel more secure ... yet more insecure at the same time; afraid, but not afraid. I've never felt like this about anybody before.

Damn, relationships are hard.

So the rest of the day I walk around with this hollow feeling in my gut about my relationship with Jennifer. It really gets to me in Social Studies, while Mr. McCoy lectures us on the human need to be social.

He shows us this totally sad, old black-and-white movie of a baby monkey separated from its mother at birth. It's clinging more to a soft piece of carpet shaped like a mother monkey than a wire one with a food bottle attached to it. According to the film, bonding is such a biological imperative that, in the absence of another living being, we'll bond to anything that provides comfort - even over food, it seems.

Why anybody would want to separate a baby monkey from its mother is beyond me. And did they really need to do that just to figure out all that stuff about bonding? Couldn't they just look around?

I realize that I need to do something to get back on the right track with Jennifer or I'm gonna go crazy. I've been doodling, like I always do when I'm distracted, and as Mr. McCoy blathers on, I decide to do a portrait of her.

I pull out my sketchbook from my school bag, but can't find any of my good sketch pencils, so I'm forced to use a regular writing one instead.

I don't usually draw people. The only time I have is when I've gotten an assignment in art class - and usually then there's a model in front of me. But when I draw Jennifer, for some reason, I'm able to recall by heart almost every line, angle, and shade of skin on her face.

I'm so involved in the drawing that I don't even hear the bell ring to end the period. I only realize the class is over when I lift my head and see that everyone's gone from the room. Mr. McCoy looks at me like I'm an idiot.

But the portrait's done. And when I finally step back and take a look at it, I'm impressed with my work. Using nothing but a Dixon Ticonderoga #2, I've managed to give Jennifer's face a glow that may or may not exist in the eyes of most people, but definitely does in mine.

I can't wait to show it to her, so I go right to her next class - Algebra - and wait for her outside the door.

"What are you doing?" she asks when she sees me.

She sounds kind of cold and for a moment I consider not telling her. But I fight my urge to chicken out and say, "Uh, I wanted to see you ... and give you this." I hand her the sketch.

She looks at it and I can't quite tell what she's

thinking, but hope they're good thoughts. In case she's still upset, I add, "I'm sorry. If you're not doing anything tonight, I really want you to come out with -"

She looks up from the sketch and interrupts me. "It's okay. You don't have to do that."

"No, really. I want to. It's just that -"

"You don't have to explain. You said you're sorry." She has this glow on her face that makes me turn to jelly. It has the completely opposite effect on one specific part of my anatomy, though. "That's enough."

"So you'll come out tonight?"

She nods and that's the end of it. She's back. Better yet, *we're* back.

It's amazing; she's so much more grown-up than any other girl I've gone out with. Definitely more than me - even though she's a junior and I'm a senior. They say girls mature faster than boys. I believe it.

She smiles and I think I see her face scrunch, like she's about to cry. She looks back at the sketch. "Nobody's ever drawn me before," she says. "It's beautiful. I love it. Thank you."

It's a great feeling when someone responds so positively to something you created. That's probably why I do it all in the first place. But nobody's ever responded this well, in this way. I like it.

She looks back up at me and again the old beams of light shoot from her face.

The school bell rings, which is probably just as well, before I screw it up somehow. "See you after school?" I ask.

This time she nods, steps forward, and gives me a kiss. It's more than the usual peck this time; this is a major PDA, right in the hallway. Tongue and everything. If I wasn't so relieved about things being back to normal, I'd be totally aroused - well, more aroused than I am, anyway.

She goes into her class, staring at the sketch. I adjust the crotch of my jeans to give me - *it* - room and smile. Jennifer and I are back - and better than ever.

As usual, at the end of the school day I meet Mike in the lobby, where everybody who drives to school gathers. Mostly it's full of student athletes getting ready for practice.

I used to be on the soccer team and run track, but that was in junior high and only for a year. It didn't take long for me to see that there wasn't much point in it, especially once I realized I wanted to go to art school. I knew I was better off with a part time job. Plus, I doubt The University of the Arts cares how fast I can run the hundred meters.

The first thing Mike says when I see him is, "There's a party at Karen Lutz's house tonight."

"Really? Karen Lutz?" Karen's the last person you'd think would throw a party. I mean, she plays saxophone in the marching band and is a catcher on the softball team. Not that there's anything wrong with those things; they just don't scream "partier."

"Well, she told me her parents are away, so ..." Mike says.

"Ah. And does *Karen* know about this party?"

Mike smiles. "She will soon enough."

I laugh, then see Jennifer. She's talking to Rick Schmidt. Rick's older than I am, richer, taller, more athletic ... basically, everything that makes you popular in high school, he's got more of. And I have to confess that I'm a little jealous of him - not so much because of all those things, but because he went out with Jennifer for a few weeks before I did. So it bothers me when I see them together, talking like they're old friends.

Mike doesn't help matters by tilting his head toward them and saying, "What's goin' on there?"

"What?" I say, like I have no idea what he's talking about.

"Jennifer and Captain Beefcake over there."

"They're friends," I say. "Whatever."

"Didn't they used to go out?"

"That doesn't mean anything."

Mike nods with fake agreement. He can probably read the fear on my face.

Man, it sucks how the littlest thing like her talking to her ex can make me doubt the whole enterprise, if only for an instant - which is, thankfully, as long as it lasts, because as soon as she sees me, she runs over, all excited.

"Oh, good. You're here. I wanted to do this this morning, but ..." she says and looks at me with a slightly sad face, I guess for the earlier difficulty, then smiles again. "Close your eyes; hold out your hands."

"Huh?"

"Just do it."

So I do.

Still, it's weird standing there with my eyes closed in the middle of a lobby full of people. But I trust her.

I can hear Jennifer walk away from me. I'm not sure where she's going, or why, but I try hard to keep my eyes closed. I don't want her to catch me opening them and get mad at me again. I doubt she would, but why risk it?

"What's she doing?" I ask Mike.

"I don't know."

Thankfully, within a minute she returns.

She puts something in my hands. "Okay. Open." Her voice is cheerful. I can hear her smiling before I open my eyes and see her face.

In my hands is a Tastykake Coconut Junior, a small, pre-packaged cake with white icing and pieces of coconut sprinkled on top. It's my favorite. I don't know how she remembered that. I love that she did, though.

There's a lit candle stuck in the middle of the cake and as it burns she sings the "Happy Birthday" song.

At first I'm embarrassed and can feel my face redden as the people around me stare. But as I look at Jennifer I can see that she's not self-conscious at all. She just sings away, without a care in the world for what anybody thinks.

I don't know how she does it - maybe it's from all the cheerleading - but the fact that she's willing to risk embarrassment for me makes me less self-conscious. I want to kiss and hug her right there. And I would if there wasn't a burning candle between us.

"Make a wish," she says after she completes the song and accepts the smattering of applause from several onlookers.

I look at her for one more moment, make my wish - which involves her, of course - and blow out the candle. Then I give her a long hug and a kiss. Fear of PDA's be damned!

As I drive home with Mike, I get a chance to finish my Coconut Junior birthday cake. It's got to be the most delicious thing I've ever eaten.

"Awww. Now wasn't that *sweet*," Mike says of the whole episode.

I detect a note of jealousy in his voice - or maybe I just want to. He's always had better luck than me when it comes to women … girls … whatever. They've all been under eighteen, so I guess they were girls. Just like I was a boy, supposedly, until I turned eighteen.

"Yes. As a matter of fact, it was sweet," I say proudly through the wad of cake in my mouth.

"Fuck sweet," he says. "Sour's way more fun."

Like Jennifer, my mom gets me a cake for my birthday. It's white with elaborate blue trim and lettering, much larger than the Coconut Junior, and my name's written on this one, inside a ring of eighteen candles.

After dinner she lights the candles and sings me a much less cheery version of "Happy Birthday" than Jennifer's. She kind of talks her way through it.

As she finishes, the doorbell rings. I figure it's Mike, ready to get the evening started, so I blow out the candles and stand to get the door.

My mom looks at me, disappointed. "Did you even make a wish?"

I shrug. I hadn't thought about it. But I go ahead and make the same wish I had before, the one that involves Jennifer, then head to the front door to greet Mike.

It's not Mike, though. It's Gary, my mom's "boyfriend." She hasn't been seeing him very long, but it's enough for me to know that I don't like him all that much. Not that he's a bad person or anything; he just always strikes me as kind of rough. Dirty, even. He's not particularly classy, either.

At the moment, he's wearing worn jeans and a faded black T-shirt under a heavy, green army jacket. I don't think he was ever in the army - or any other branch of the service, for that matter. But I don't know.

His hands are blackened from his job as a lineman for the phone company. I think that's what he does ... or maybe it's the power company ... something like that. He hasn't even shaved.

This *is how you come to see my mom?*

Really, though, the thing that bothers me most about him is that he tries too hard to get me to like him. I hate when guys do that ... like it's gonna make me okay with the idea of them doing my mom - which I can only assume is happening.

"Hey, Bri," he says, all enthusiastic. "How ya doin'?"

"All right," I mumble and walk back to the kitchen, him on my tail the whole way. "It's only Gary."

My mom seems surprised. "Oh, hi. You're early." He kisses her and she downplays it, probably because it's in front of me.

He must read her discomfort, because he says, "I'm sorry. Am I interrupting? I can leave if you want."

"Don't be silly. Sit. Are you hungry?" She grabs a plate and sets it in front of him before he can answer.

The doorbell rings again. This time it has to be Mike.

I jump right up, eager to get away from being forced to watch Gary eat. It's not a pretty sight. I can't believe my mom can even stand it. She used to tear my head off when I opened my mouth with food in it. Now she's dating a guy who chews like a horse eating an apple covered with peanut butter.

"I'll get it," my mom says. "Sit. Eat. Cut your cake."

I do as I'm told, but before my mom can leave the

room to greet him, Mike invites himself in like he has since he was a little kid and strolls into the kitchen.

He sees me cutting the cake. "Hey! What is this?! A party?! And I wasn't invited? Mrs. H, I'm hurt."

"Come in, Mike," my mom says with a laugh and shake of her head. "Have some cake."

"No time, Mrs. H. Gotta roll."

"Oh, you have time for some cake. Now sit."

"Yes, Ma'am," Mike says with forced humility and sits.

He looks at Gary, as if he's just now noticed something different in the picture. There are *never* other people in the house with my mom and me - let alone an adult male.

Once I see the look on Mike's face, I also realize how strange Gary's presence is. I wonder why that is - and why I hadn't noticed before.

"Mike, this is Gary," my mom says.

The two nod hello. Mike looks back and forth between Gary and my mom. I can see him doing the math. He shoots me a funny look as my mom puts a piece of cake in front of him.

"So ... Gary," Mike says with a big smile, "how do you know Mrs. Hartman?"

Gary looks at him a moment, then at my mom. He seems unsure how to answer. "We're ... dating," he says, although it sounds kind of like a question. My mom nods to confirm it.

"I see. And are your intentions ... honorable?"

"Now don't be a smart ass, Mike," my mom says.

I laugh. "Yeah. Don't be a smart ass."

"What?" Mike says and tries to look like he didn't mean anything by it. "I'm just talking."

With a knowing look on her face, my mom turns Mike's chin back toward his plate. "Eat your cake."

He shrugs, gulps down his cake in two bites, stands, and turns to me. "Awright, Bro, let's rock and roll."

I jump at the chance to get out of the house.

"Sure you don't want to take my car tonight?" my mom says. She'd probably prefer it if I drove. I think she trusts me more than she does Mike. I suppose she should - and not just because she's my mom.

"Now what kind of friend would I be if I made him drive on his birthday?" Mike says and pulls me out of the room.

"Be careful!" my mom yells after us.

As we get into his car, Mike says, "So ... Gary, eh?"

I don't feel like explaining, so I just shrug.

"They, uh ...?" Mike makes a fist and pushes the air a few times with it.

"I don't know. Just drive," I say. I don't want to think about it. "Oh, and we gotta pick up Jennifer."

"What?! You serious?"

I nod.

"Yer such a puss ..." Mike shakes his head in disgust and reaches for a bottle of soda from his cup holder.

Before he can get it to his lips, I stop him and sniff the bottle. It's definitely not straight Mountain Dew. Smells like vodka, too.

"Just pre-gamin' a little," he says.

I grab the bottle from him, put the cap back on, and return it to the cup holder. I then look at him to make sure he's sober enough to drive. He looks okay and the bottle's still full, so I figure he's fine.

He shakes his head. "You're getting pussier and

pussier every day, you know that?"

I wave for him to forget it and start driving, which he does, but not without a smirk and a sigh.

Mike and I pick up Jennifer and go straight to Karen Lutz's house. There are already a few people there when we arrive, which is surprising because usually when it comes to these things Mike is like the Marines: first one in, last one out.

Since it's usually his party, no matter where it's held, he feels a special responsibility to keep the nervous host distracted while her parents' house swells with people. Then once the ball begins to roll and will continue on its own, he can sit back and enjoy the ride. At Karen's house, it isn't long before he grabs a bottle of vodka from her parents' liquor cabinet, pours some into a shaker with other things he's found, and plays bartender.

Meanwhile, Karen roams the house trying to keep things under control. She sees what Mike's up to and says, "Hey. That's my dad's."

"Relax, Karen. Here, have a drink." Mike pours four shots and hands three of them to Karen, me, and Jennifer.

Jennifer waves hers off. She's not much of a drinker. Neither am I, really. If anything, I'm a *one-and-done* kind of drinker. Or maybe *two-and-I'm-through*, at best. I guess that's because it's never been a forbidden fruit to me the way it is to some people.

My mother knew that if I wanted to drink alcohol, I would - and there was nothing she could do about it with how little she was around. Plus, on the rare occasions that she actually had a drink, she'd let me taste it, so I never thought it was anything special.

"Oh, loosen up, Jenny," Mike says. "It's Brian's birthday."

I step in. "Mike, she doesn't want it."

Mike smirks, shakes his head, and holds up his glass. "Here's to the crack that never heals," he begins to toast. "The more you rub it the better -"

"Whoa, whoa, whoa!" I look at Mike and shake my head. It's pretty crude what he's saying ... and it only gets worse from there.

I know Mike likes to say things like that to prove he's mature or to shock people or something. And I don't really care because I'm used to it. But Jennifer's not and like with the magazine, I don't want her to think that's the kind of person I am.

"All right. Whatever," Mike mumbles with disgust. "To my Brother from another mother. Happy Birthday, Buddy." He puts his arm around me and downs the drink. Karen cringes as she drinks hers. I sip half of mine, pour the rest in the sink when Mike's not looking, and wink at Jennifer.

Mike drinks the fourth shot, puts his other arm around Karen, and says, "There ya go. See? I'm putting the booze away. Your dad'll never notice."

Just then, Tracy Bowman passes and catches Mike's eye. Tracy's a senior. Very good looking. Homecoming Queen material. She was actually in the court, but didn't win.

I have to fight not to look at her, myself. Not that I think she's prettier than Jennifer, but like Mike says, boys will be boys.

The music playing in the other room gets louder. Karen frowns and leaves to deal with it. When she's gone, Mike pulls the bottle of vodka out again, smiles, and follows Tracy.

I turn to Jennifer and shake my head at Mike the same way my mom does when he misbehaves. His hijinks are harmless.

She smiles at me. "I have something for you."

"Really?"

She nods, takes my hand, and leads me out. You can guess what I think she might have for me. Well, I'm not sure ... but I hope it's something pretty good.

Jennifer leads me upstairs and into one of the empty bedrooms of Karen's house. It's clearly a child's room - a younger brother of Karen's, probably - because there's a baseball mural on the wall, baseball-themed bedspread, and a small chair in the shape of a baseball glove.

We sit on the bed and I'm not sure what's going to happen, but I have a few ideas of what I *want* to happen. I didn't make those two birthday wishes for nothing.

Maybe it's the décor, but I'm thinking Home Run. I doubt that would happen here in a strange room, in a strange house, especially for the first time, but a double or stand-up triple would be nice. Better than nice.

Excited by the prospect, I lean in to kiss her, but as I do she turns, pulls out a gift-wrapped box from her purse, and hands it to me.

"Oh," I say.

"What?"

"Nothing. I just ... Um, you didn't have to do this."

"I know. But I wanted to."

I hide my disappointment and see this for what it is: a very nice gesture. My body releases any remaining expectation of physical contact and I force myself to focus on the gift. It's not easy.

I rip off the gift wrap to reveal a long, wooden case. Inside is a set of very fine Winsor & Newton Sable paintbrushes. They're really good artist's brushes. She had to have done some research to know. And spent some serious cash.

"Wow."

"Are they okay?" she asks. "The guy at the store said they were the best they had."

"Um, yeah ... they're, they're ... great ... thank you."

It's a very considerate and generous gift. The mere thought of it brings back the warm feeling in my body. I can't control my impulse to kiss her.

So I do.

Mmmm, does she taste good. I've never tasted any other girl like her before. It's fantastic.

We make out for a little and slowly become more turned on - at least I know *I* do.

At one point I rub her chest, unbutton her top, pull her bra aside, and even manage to put my mouth on her breast. She seems to like it, but after a minute pulls away.

I may have overreached, trying to steal second like that - with my mouth, no less - but what can I say? So I got lost in the moment ... not such a bad thing, right? Hopefully she understands that it's because I like being with her. I *really* like being with her. But I said that already.

After that, we go back to kissing. I don't push the physical stuff anymore, and it's okay. The last thing I want to do is risk losing her by moving too fast.

But, boy, I'd like to keep going.

We eventually return to the party and mingle with the others, who are all wearing hats now. Not the same kind, like party hats or something, though; each is different. It turns out Mr. Bowman has a hat collection and there's one kid with a stack of them who's handing them out to people.

I feel bad for Karen, who didn't sign up for this much chaos in her parents' house. Still, it's hysterical to see, especially since everybody seems to take on the character of their respective headgear. Like, one girl in a cowboy hat is waving her arm and yelling, "Yee-hah!" while a guy in a beret makes a snooty face and speaks with a bad French accent and yet another guy in a Viking helmet struts around with his chest out, grunting. There's a kid in a coonskin cap, another in a priest hat, and another in a puffy chef toque - which I know the proper name for from my job working in a kitchen.

Just about every hat you can think of is represented in some form and when the kid who's handing out the collection sees that Jennifer and I aren't wearing any, he puts an astronaut helmet on me and a red velvet fez on her. We look at each other and laugh. I put my hands on my hips, turn my head, and look off and up, as if to the sky. There's not much she can do to model her hat for me but just look cute. And she does - totally.

For a while we interact with everybody, but mostly stay close to each other and even dance a little. She's a really good dancer and just watching her makes me ache to be closer to her. And I'm not just talking about sex - although I'm sure that's part of it; I am eighteen, after all.

There's definitely something else at work, though, and

I steal every possible kiss I can, wherever I can, without regard for who's watching. In fact, I barely even notice anyone else, I'm so lost in her company. I think she's lost in mine, too - at least until she checks the time and panics when she realizes it's almost midnight. That's her curfew.

We search the house like crazy to find Mike, so he can drive her home - that is, if he's in any shape to drive. I'm pretty sure he's been drinking, so most likely I'll be doing the driving.

"Anybody seen Mike Welch?" I ask a bunch of people. Nobody has, not for a while.

Jennifer looks more and more nervous as it approaches midnight. Even if we find Mike right away, at this point there's no way she's not going to be late getting home.

"Wait here," I say in the kitchen. "I'll find him." I run upstairs and search the bedrooms. I think maybe Mike is with someone - probably Tracy - and I don't want Jennifer to see ... for the same reason I didn't want her to hear the toast earlier ... or see the porn magazine Mike brought to school.

"Mike! Hey Mike!" I yell inside each room.

At the last of the bedrooms, I open the door, turn on the light, and there he is, with Tracy, on the bed. They're making out, but their clothes are still on - thankfully. In fact, it looks like they just started kissing.

Mike squints at me. "Dude. What're you doing?"

"We gotta go."

"What? No. Why?"

"Jennifer was supposed to be home by midnight."

"So? Take her home."

"Okay. Gimme your keys."

He fumbles in his pockets for his car keys. I can tell he's drunk.

Tracy looks embarrassed - probably for being caught

making out. "I should be going, too," she says and peels herself away from Mike.

He tugs at her arm. "Aw, you don't have to leave yet."

She laughs and shakes her arm loose.

"At least give me your number." She stops and gives him her phone number, which he repeats out loud as he takes out his phone and programs it in. She smiles coyly as she walks past me, out the door.

After Mike finishes putting Tracy's number in his phone, he stares at me. "Bro ... what the hell ... ?"

I can only shrug apologetically and say, "Hey, at least you got her digits," as I lead him downstairs to Jennifer and the car outside.

He continues to complain all the way, despite my attempts to keep him quiet. "You're killin' me over here. Y'know I'm gonna have to sleep on my back tonight ... and it's all your fault."

"Just get in the car," I say and hold out my hand for the keys.

"I'll drive."

"No you won't."

"What? I'm fine. Look." He touches his nose and walks what he thinks is a straight line. "See?"

I smirk and say, "Okay," but when he takes out his keys I snatch them from him and push him in the back seat. I let Jennifer in the passenger side and drive her home as quickly as I can.

As soon as the car screeches to a halt in front of Jennifer's house, she kisses me and hops out. "Call me tomorrow."

I nod and say, "Thanks for the brushes ... I love them," after her.

She looks back and smiles, just as her father - at least I assume he's her father; I've never met him - appears out of nowhere next to the car. It's like he just returned from another dimension or something.

He's not at all what I expected. He's kind of short, with this geeky, slicked-back haircut and stern look on his face that's probably there even when he's happy - which he definitely is not at the moment.

Mike practically jumps through the roof of the car. "Jesus Christ! Where the hell did he come from?!"

I shoot Mike a "shut the hell up" look and get out of the car.

"Dad, I'm sorry. I -" Jennifer starts to say before I interrupt.

"I'm sorry, Mr. Kinney. I know it's late. It's all my fault. See, it was my birthday and we went -"

He doesn't want to hear it. "Go inside, Jennifer."

She takes one last sad look at me and drags her feet toward the house.

Mr. Kinney stares at me until she's inside. The second the door closes, he says, "What's your name?"

"Brian."

"Right. Brian," he says as if writing my name down in a police report. He looks at Mike, sizes him up, and smirks before turning back to me.

"Look, Brian ... if you want to see my daughter, you're going to have to follow the rules."

"'Rules'?" Mike says. "There are *rules* now?"

"Um, I'm sorry," I say to cut Mike off, "I was just trying -"

"I know what you were trying. It's my job to keep you from succeeding."

Again, Mike pipes up. "Suck. Seed. Heh-heh."

I roll my eyes and again look at Mr. Kinney apologetically - for both keeping Jennifer out and now for being friends with the drunk in the back seat.

Mr. Kinney squints at me, like he's psychically warning me to stay out of trouble - or, at the very least, out of his daughter - and walks away.

I turn back to Mike. "What the hell are you doing to me?"

"I'm sorry, Bro. I was just -" Mike's face curls. "Uh-oh."

I've seen this look before. And I know what's coming.

I step back from the car just as Mike leans out and pukes all over the street.

A perfect end to the night, I think - although I really can't complain. It was pretty good up until Mr. Kinney showed up, what with the gift Jennifer gave me and getting to second base.

Then I realize it's not my birthday anymore. It's well after midnight - and that's when things went south.

So, all in all, it was a pretty good eighteenth birthday.

SECOND

The morning after my birthday, I ride my bicycle to Adult World, lock it up behind the store, look around to make sure no one can see me, and go inside to work. Tommy and Mr. Welch are there.

"There he is," Mr. Welch says with a smile and looks at his watch. "Five minutes early, too."

I take off my winter coat to reveal my Truman's outfit, a shirt and tie.

"We're not Truman's, Brian," Mr. Welch says with a laugh, "You don't need to wear a tie here. Tommy, get him a staff shirt."

Tommy goes in the back.

"That's okay. You don't have to waste one on me," I say.

"It won't be a waste."

Tommy returns and tosses a shirt to me. I'd be skeeved if it was a used shirt, but from the way it smells and isn't frayed, I can tell it's brand new, so I don't mind wearing it.

I take off my shirt and tie and put it on. It's a little big, but since I figure I'm only gonna wear it for one day, I don't worry about it.

"Okay, Brian, my boy," Mr. Welch says as he puts his hand on my shoulder and begins a tour of the store. "Rule Number One: In here, anything goes. There are no subjects out of bounds. Got it? These people make the effort to come here - sometimes literally - so we don't want them to feel ashamed about it. No matter what they say, make like it's the most normal thing in the world. Some guy asks if we have any videos with, I don't know, people pissing on each other -"

My face curls with incomprehension. *Is he kidding me?* One look at his face tells me he's not.

"Right. We don't want to look at him - or her - that way. Remember, this is all legal. There's nothing for anyone to be ashamed of. It may be unusual, but it's just business ... and I'm a businessman. So if we have a video like that -"

"Do you?"

"I think so ... in the foreign section. Probably German. Those bastards are crazy. Anyway, if we do have it, show him. Take him there if you have to, but don't linger. Let him do his own thing. If we don't have it, suggest something close to it. It's -"

Mr. Welch stops as a skinny guy with messy hair enters the store and takes off his coat to reveal an Adult World staff shirt. He doesn't seem much older than I am - probably early to mid-twenties - and looks like he just woke up or is hung-over or something.

"Robby," Mr. Welch says, "you're late."

"Sorry, Boss. I'll make it up."

"Times two. This ain't a charity."

Robby nods humbly and gets to work.

"I guess it went okay last night?" Mr. Welch asks him.

Robby nods, reaches into his pocket.

"That's okay. We'll take care of it later." Mr. Welch turns back to me for an introduction. "Brian, Robby. Robby, Brian."

I nod hello. Robby nods back, sizes me up, then looks at Tommy, who shrugs.

A customer enters the store. He has that look people get on their face when they wish they could make themselves invisible. His eyes are down and his face is blank as he heads back to the room where the booths are.

"And don't worry about anything in there," Mr. Welch says. "I got a guy who comes in, collects the money from the machines and cleans. Otherwise, it's all self-service." He winks and pats me on the shoulder, again in that fatherly way. I'm beginning to like it. "Low overhead's what it's all about in business, Brian. Low overhead. You remember that."

I nod. I will remember that. I'm not sure exactly what it means, or how it'll apply to my life as an artist, but I can certainly use all the life lessons I can get.

A half hour or so later, the store fills up with customers in anticipation of Rita Hanson's appearance.

Between taking phone calls, dealing with store issues, or talking with Tommy and Robby, Mr. Welch has basically told me what he expects me to do all day. What he doesn't get a chance to tell me I can pretty much figure out by following him and watching what the other employees do.

I'm a pretty fast learner that way. As long as I can see someone do something, I can usually figure it out, or at least mimic it enough to get by until I do. That's what you do when you don't have someone around all the time to teach you things; you figure them out on your own. And so far I haven't seen anything too complicated going on in the store.

At one point I'm standing behind the register with Mr. Welch and Tommy when a customer approaches.

"I got this one, Tommy," Mr. Welch says, then turns to me and nods toward the cash register. "Brian, let me show you how this works."

I've worked a much more complex register at Truman's for years, so I figure the pretty basic one they use at Adult World should be a breeze. Plus, I've seen Tommy ring a few things up already.

"I got it," I say.

Mr. Welch looks at me, impressed. "Go 'head, then."

I greet the customer like I would a typical grocery store shopper. And really, what's the difference between buying a carton of eggs, a quart of milk, or a pound of butter and a few porn videos, a rubber penis, or a pair of faux-fur covered handcuffs? Well, nutritional value, I suppose ... but otherwise, it's just stuff.

So I ring the guy up, take his money, put it in the register, and bag his purchase - which in this case is a video, some lubrication jelly, and something that looks like a string of beads. I'm not sure what it is or what it's for. I'm pretty sure it's not a necklace, though.

Mr. Welch smiles and nods at me. "How 'bout the kid? Eh, Tommy?" Tommy shrugs. He seems to shrug a lot.

"Thank you," I say to the customer. "Come again." I laugh like a little kid as I realize the double meaning of what I say here and have said all the time at Truman's.

Before leaving, the customer turns to Mr. Welch and asks, "Do you rent videos, too?"

Mr. Welch directs his attention to me and prods me to answer.

But I'm not sure yet. "Do you?" I ask.

"No. *We* don't," he says. "Just for purchase. And believe me, you're better off." He looks at the man with a knowing eyebrow-raise. "You really wanna get a video after some guy's taken it home?"

The customer seems to consider it.

"Seriously. Go to one of those rental places with a black light someday - the place'll glow like the back of a Spencer Gifts store."

I fight laughter as the customer cringes.

"Exactly. And the Internet?" Mr. Welch adds. "With all the identity issues, government tracking you, all that ... to say nothing of all the viruses. Trust me, you wanna come in here and *buy*. We don't ask and you don't have to tell," he says, with a wink. "Plus, here, your satisfaction is guaranteed."

The customer nods and exits.

When he's gone, Mr. Welch laughs and turns to me. "Heh. I've never had to make good on *that* guarantee."

"No?"

"Would *you* want to admit something like that?"

I smile. "No, I guess not."

He puts his hand on my shoulder. "Well, I think you got this pretty much under control. Any questions, ask Tommy."

I look at Tommy and nod.

"Good boy." Mr. Welch ruffles my hair, then yells for Robby, who's working the floor, stocking shelves. He tilts his head toward the back. Robby stops what he's doing and follows Mr. Welch into the back room.

At around noon, the store's pretty full and we're all busy working. There's another man, Charlie, who I'd guess is in his sixties and dressed in clothes he's probably owned for thirty years, now helping us out. I say "helping us out" because he doesn't really work at Adult World; he just comes in a lot, apparently.

"Don't ask me why …" Robby says, then goes on to explain that maybe it's for the old inventory that Mr. Welch gives him sometimes.

As I watch Charlie work with - and try to engage - the others, I get the feeling he's a lonely man and does it more because he enjoys the company. He's not wearing a wedding ring and doesn't mention a wife or girlfriend or anything, so I don't know what his story is. But he seems like a nice enough person, if a little strange.

I help him set up a table and chair for the guest of honor when she arrives, while Tommy and Robby argue over what movie to play in the store.

"*Great Sexpectations.*"

"How about *Sweet and Sour Porked?*"

"I'm the manager," Tommy says, "and I say *Great Sexpectations.*"

"C'mon. I don't wanna see that again. I want something good, something new. And this one looks funny."

Charlie steps in. "Can I recommend something?"

They both turn to him and say, "No."

"I was just gonna say *Lawrence of a Labia* … or *Wet Rainbow*, maybe … a classic … old school filmmaking. But go ahead, watch that new crap," Charlie mumbles.

Tommy shakes off the distraction from Charlie and

says to Robby, "Okay, we'll settle this *Rock, Paper, Scissors* style. Best of three."

Robby nods and they shoot two fast. Tommy does Scissors, then Paper. Robby does Rock each time.

"*Great Sexpectations* it is," Robby says.

"What are you talking about? We have to shoot again."

"I already won two."

"No, you didn't."

"Rock breaks Scissors, holds down Paper. Two. Duh." Robby looks at Tommy like he's an idiot.

Tommy returns the look. "Are you dense? Paper covers Rock."

"That's stupid. Rock holds down Paper, like a paperweight."

"Then Rock would always win."

"Right," Robby says. "That's why I pick it."

"Don't be an idiot. If Rock won every time there'd be no game. Everything's got to beat at least one other thing. We gotta shoot a third."

Mr. Welch comes out from the back and watches as Tommy shoots Scissors, Robby Paper.

"There. I beat you," Tommy says.

"No, you beat *it*."

"Clever." Tommy goes to put the winning video on.

"What're you two doing?" Mr. Welch asks.

"Just putting in a movie."

Mr. Welch looks at his watch. "She's gonna be here any minute. You gotta put *hers* in. Here."

Tommy looks at the box. "*The Starlet?*" he says. "This is terrible."

"Yeah," Robby chimes in. "Too much story. Like she's some kind of 'actress'. Don't talk, baby. Just suck it or spread it; there's your direction."

I laugh. It's fun to watch them talk like that.

"When I was a kid -" Charlie starts to say before he's interrupted by the groans and eye rolls of the others.

Tommy and Robby, as if on cue, both say "Here we go ..." and scatter.

Charlie then directs his speech at me. I have no choice but to listen.

"When I was a kid, we didn't need all this stuff," he says. "Mechanical vaginas, battery-operated stroke machines, anal -"

I fear he's going to tell me a little too much about himself ... stuff I'm either not willing - or perhaps even ready - to hear.

Thankfully, Mr. Welch runs interference for me. "Charlie, leave him alone."

"We're just talking," Charlie says, then looks at me. "Right?"

"Um," I say, not sure what to do. I don't want to be rude, but I don't want him to go where I think he was going, either.

"Charlie's kind of a porn historian," Mr. Welch explains. "Aren't you, Charlie? Has one of the biggest collections you've ever seen. Even used to make some, right?"

Charlie nods and his speech takes on a more scholarly tone. "A long time ago. In those days it was little eight-millimeter films. *Film.* You could touch it, hold it up to the light, see through it. You had to *work* to create something. Now, any punk with a video camera does it. Where's the artistry? Where's the love?"

"We're talking about porn, Charlie. Love's got nothing to do with it," Robby says.

"Exactly. That's the problem."

"All right, everybody, break it up," Mr. Welch says

and looks at the door as Rita Hanson enters. "Here she comes."

"I'm sure she hasn't come in years ..." Tommy says under his breath.

Rita approaches and says a bunch of flirty hellos to us all. She seems taken aback by me for a second - maybe it's my age - but quickly shrugs it off.

I'm taken aback by her, in return - and not because she's the first porn actress I've ever met in my life, but because she looks a lot different than the obviously very airbrushed photo of her on the poster hanging in the store. It's also clear that she's much older now than whenever the photo was taken. But she's no different than any other advertised product, I suppose. The image is always different than the reality.

The one thing I notice when she gets closer to us is that she smells a lot like one of those plug-in air fresheners. She must have over-applied the body spray.

"Hi, Ms. Hanson," Mr. Welch says, although the tone of his voice seems less respectful than calling someone "Ms." would imply. "Good to see you again. I'm Mike."

"Yes. Of course," she says, with a similar level of phoniness. "Mike. I remember."

"We have a room set up for you in the back," Mr. Welch says, "if you need it."

"That's okay. Let's just get into it."

Mr. Welch guides Rita to the table and chair Charlie set up earlier, as the customers eager to see her form a loose line and one by one approach with video boxes to autograph. She flirts with each of them as she signs.

The whole store is preoccupied with her. The only one who seems not to care one way or the other is Mr. Welch. I think he only cares about the amount of merchandise he sells. He looks happy because not only do the people buy

Rita's video, but they also pick up a variety of other items it's hard to believe anyone would want to buy - or be seen buying.

But these guys all scarf the stuff up like it's no big deal. Many don't even seem embarrassed about it. Either that or they're pretty good at hiding their shame.

But then again, shame probably depends on the circumstances. If you're caught with a video of "Lesbian Sinners of Sodom" or a "Harlots for Harness" magazine in church or school - or, hell, anywhere other than a place like Adult World - it'd probably be a big deal.

But here ... not so much.

For the next few hours I continue to work hard for Mr. Welch because, frankly, I don't care much about Rita - I mean, other than the standard curiosity.

I think Mr. Welch likes, maybe even respects, that I'm not distracted by her presence. And I like that he likes it. He winks and pats me on the shoulder again as I ring up customers.

When the hubbub is finally over, Rita asks Mr. Welch for a place to "freshen up."

"Tommy, take Miss Hanson in the back," Mr. Welch says. A sly smile forms on Tommy's face as he moves from behind the counter. Even I get the joke - although Mr. Welch probably didn't mean it that way.

"Need a hand?" Robby whispers to him.

"That's okay. I got it," Tommy says, then with a louder voice says, "Right this way ..." to Rita.

She follows him toward the back room. "So what do you think of my movie?"

"Oh, it's great. In fact, we were all just talking about it before you came."

"So you'll push it?"

"Of course," Tommy says. "Definitely." He smiles at her as he allows her to walk through the back door, then looks at us and shrugs.

The look on his face tells me there's something weird going on - or about to go on, but I don't have time to think any more about it. It's getting late and I need to get to Truman's.

"Mr. Welch, I better get going if I'm gonna make it to my other job on time," I say.

Robby turns to me. "If it's a *job* you're looking for ..."

"Don't listen to him, Brian," Mr. Welch says and shakes his head at Robby. He takes a money clip from his pocket and peels fifty dollars from it. He looks at me an extra couple of seconds, smiles, then takes another twenty and hands it all to me.

"Um, I think you said 'fifty'," I say.

"I know what I said," Mr. Welch responds with a wink. "Call it a bonus. Not bad for a few hours of work, eh?"

He puts the money clip back in his pocket and turns away so I won't argue with him further. "Oh, and here, take a copy of her film." He picks up one of Rita's movies from the small pile left on the table and hands it to me.

"Um, no, thanks. You don't have to -" I say. I don't really want it. I saw enough while it played on the TV. Plus, I don't want my mom to find it if I bring it home.

"Brian. Rule Number One: Take whatever people offer you."

The way he says it gives me no other choice but to nod and accept the video. I put it in my backpack and start to take off my Adult World staff shirt.

Mr. Welch stops me. "So, Brian, my boy, whaddya think about working for me on a more permanent basis?"

I was afraid he might ask that, from the way he watched me work earlier. Maybe I shouldn't have done such a good job. "Well, I, uh … I don't know. My other job and all …" I say.

"We can work around Truman's. We're open twenty-four hours on weekends, y'know."

I'm still not sure.

"Did I hear Mike say you're looking to buy a car?" Mr. Welch says.

I nod. I have been looking to buy a car, but not too seriously. I know it'll cost me a lot, especially since once I buy it, I'll need to pay for gas, insurance, maintenance, whatever.

"I can help you with that," he says.

I'm not sure what he means, but assume he's talking about money, which is pretty nice. And the seventy bucks in my hand is looking pretty good, too. "Well," I say, "I guess I could use a little extra -"

"Great," Mr. Welch says. Then, while he's got me on the ropes, he adds, "Why don't you come in tomorrow, same time."

"Oh, uh, okay. I guess I can do that." I feel like maybe I shouldn't, but I need money. And if here's where I gotta get it …

He nods, pats me on the back one last time, and says, "Welcome to the Adult World family."

As I walk out the door I turn around to see Tommy return from the back, smiling. He nods to Robby, who then goes back, himself. I can't help wondering what's going on.

In contrast to Adult World, my job at Truman's is now more boring and repetitive than ever. Back in my shirt and tie, I'm stuck stocking toilet paper or bagging groceries or collecting carts or doing any one of a million dull tasks I have to so I can earn my meager hourly wage.

At one point, while I'm stacking apples in that little pyramid you see in every supermarket produce aisle, Dave, the store manager, passes by.

"Brian, my man, how are you today?" he says.

I want to say that I'm bored as hell and that I wish something exciting would happen so I don't have to keep watching the clock as the minutes tick slowly by and the energy of my youth is drained to illuminate the green fluorescent overhead lights, but I don't. I don't want to complain, especially to Dave. He's a good guy. At least he's always been all right to me. I mean, he's my boss and he tells me what to do and he maybe takes his manager thing a little too seriously, but that's his job, right?

So I say, "Good," as cheerfully as I can muster.

"Another day, another dollar, eh?" he says and continues on.

I nod as I reach back into the apple box to get a new brick for the pyramid. The soft, rotten apple I pick up leaves a cider stink on my hand that takes an hour to fade away.

It makes me think maybe putting dirty movies up on a store shelf for more money might not be such a bad thing after all and I feel better about my decision to work at Adult World - although it wasn't much of my decision, now that I look back on it.

The next day at Adult World is better than the first, mostly because Tommy warms up to me. It's only the two of us working and the store is busier than you'd think for a Sunday afternoon, although there seem to be more men in the booth side than the merchandise side. I comment on it to Tommy, who tells me it's always like that on Sundays.

"Beats going to church, I guess," he says. "Hell, for some of 'em it *is* church. They're here *everyday*. With what they spend they could get an *actual* woman."

"So why come here?" I ask.

"Got tired of coming at home." Tommy chuckles once, more to himself than anything, then shrugs. "Eh, it's the same reason people go to the movies, watch television, whatever: It's clean."

"'Clean'?" I say. "I don't know about that ..."

"I mean *easy*."

I look at him like I don't know what he's talking about - because I don't.

Without looking, he points to the television, where a movie's playing. In it, a man and a woman are having sex against a piano, the keys making random sounds each time he thrusts. "When was the last time your car broke down by a farm and the farmer's daughters both fucked you?" he says. "Or you delivered a pizza to a house that turned out to be a brothel having a dick-sucking contest? Real women are never that easy. Hell, *Life*'s never that easy. Life bites ..."

I watch the movie another few minutes and think about what he's said ... and why. Is life harder after school, when you're Tommy's age? I thought it was supposed to get easier. I thought things got simpler, clearer. I hope I'm not wrong.

Right after the man and woman pound the final note on the piano in the movie, the front door opens and two women, a brunette and a redhead, enter the store. They look like they're somewhere in their thirties, although it's always hard for me to tell a thing like that. The one thing I can tell is that the brunette is shy, embarrassed, even, about being in the store. The redhead doesn't seem to care and I think is just happy to look around the place.

Out of the side of his mouth, Tommy says, "Vibrator."

I look at the women to see if I can tell how he might know that, but I have no clue. "Yeah?"

He nods and points to the quieter of the two, the brunette. "The friend, the fun one, is along with her for support, to make it not so weird."

"How do you know?"

"Trust me."

We both watch as the women move throughout the store, speaking to each other in hushed tones, although occasionally the redhead bursts into laughter, only to be shushed by the brunette. It's fun to watch and definitely a breath of fresh air in the otherwise stale environment.

"Two types of women come in here," Tommy whispers, "the kind that are curious and the kind that come with a purpose ... or with the purpose of coming, I should say."

Sure enough, the brunette works her way to the sex toy area and zeroes in on the vibrators.

"What'd I tell you?" Tommy says.

I laugh as I watch the redhead join her friend and yell, "There ya go!"

The brunette shoots her a look to tell her to be quiet, but it only seems to incite her friend to have more fun at her expense. She points to the largest vibrator on the wall display. "Oh, that one looks like it'll give you the workout you're looking for."

"Stop it!" the brunette says and looks around to make sure no one is paying attention. Tommy and I are, but we try not to look like it.

At the same time, a man who has just entered and is walking toward the booths stops when he hears the women's voices. He looks, sees them, and hides his face as much as he can behind the collar of his coat like a criminal doing a perp walk. The women snicker and whisper to each other as they watch him disappear into the booth area.

The brunette checks out a few more vibrators, selects a rather large one, and drifts casually toward the register with her friend.

"Have you sold any vibrators yet?" Tommy asks me before they get there.

"No."

He smiles wide. "Watch this."

I step away and look busy so the brunette won't feel any more uncomfortable than she already does, and watch the redhead continue on toward the booth side.

"Where you going?" the brunette asks.

"I wanna go see." The redhead turns to me. "I can go back there, right?"

I don't see why not, but still look at Tommy to make sure. He nods, so I say, "Sure. Help yourself."

"I just might," she says with a suggestive smile. I laugh and look at Tommy, who's watching her. I think he likes her. She smiles at him and continues back.

Tommy returns to the brunette customer, holds out the vibrator she's buying, and says, "You sure this is the one you want?" which seems a little inconsiderate of her situation. I'm sure the last thing she wants to do is admit that it's for her. She'd probably like to at least pretend it's a purchase for someone else.

Still, Tommy waits for her answer before he continues to ring her up.

She looks confused, but finally nods as I wonder why she's buying a vibrator in the first place. She's kind of pretty, if in a quiet way, and I'm sure could easily get a guy.

But then again, maybe she doesn't want one. Or maybe she's a lesbian and the redhead is her partner. But I didn't get that feeling from them.

There are a million possibilities, I suppose: she might have just gotten out of a relationship. Maybe she got hurt by someone. Or maybe the guy died ... or just left. Maybe it was abusive and she doesn't want to risk being back in a situation like that. Or maybe it's just that this is easier, like Tommy said before about the movies.

Relationships - real, interpersonal relationships - aren't easy, as I'm starting to learn all too well. So sometimes it's probably just less hassle to get yourself off and keep the human complications out of it.

And this vibrator looks like it'll do the job for her.

"You sure?" Tommy repeats. "I want you to get the one that's right for you."

She's a little thrown by his nonchalance. "Um, is, is that one ... not good?"

"Oh, yeah, it's fine. Is this your first?"

She nods again, even more embarrassed, and looks for her friend, who's still in the back.

Tommy glances at me with a knowing smile and says, "You're sure, then?" when the woman turns back to him.

She looks confused, but nods anyway.

"Okay." Tommy begins to open the package.

"What're you ... what are you doing?" the woman says.

"I have to check to make sure it works."

"Um, no, that's okay. I'm sure it does."

"No. Really. It's the law."

"The law?"

"Yeah," Tommy says. "Since you can't return it, I have to make sure it's going to work for you."

She squints suspiciously. "That's not true."

He nods, opens the battery chamber on the vibrator, puts two large batteries inside, and closes it. "Y'know, 'cause of hygiene, health codes, and all ..."

She looks at me to confirm what Tommy's saying. I try to nod as convincingly as I can, even though I have no idea what he's talking about.

Tommy looks at the woman, says, "See?" and turns on the vibrator. The loud whirr it makes fills the otherwise quiet store and the woman flinches from the noise.

The redhead hurries out of the booth area and looks at Tommy, who waves the running vibrator in the air at various angles, which gives its noise different pitches. "Jesus Christ!" she says with a laugh. "I thought for a second you were drilling a tooth out here!" She laughs even louder. "I guess we're talking about a whole different kind of cavity, though, huh?"

Tommy laughs.

The brunette looks like she wants to run from the store. I feel for her. This experience is clearly much more embarrassing than she expected it to be.

Tommy runs the vibrator for a few uncomfortable moments more and finally turns it off. "Okay. It's in tip-top shape."

"That'll keep you smiling, eh, Kel?" the redhead says and shares a smile with Tommy.

He repackages the vibrator, finishes ringing up the order, and hands Kel, or Kelly, or whatever her name is, the bag.

"There ya go. Enjoy. And come again." He smiles, turns to the redhead, and gives her a friendly look. "You too."

She returns his smile warmly as the brunette, who is only too happy to get the hell out of the store, says, "Let's go," and yanks her out the door.

As they leave, since I'm nearer to the entrance than Tommy, I can hear the redhead say, "What are you doing? He's cute."

The brunette responds with, "What are you, nuts? He works in a porn - " but the door closes before she can finish.

When they're gone, Tommy smiles to himself and goes back to work. I don't think he heard the brunette, which is good. I get the feeling if this were any other kind of store he'd have had a shot with the redhead. It was clear there was something between the two of them.

It's funny what he did to the brunette with the vibrator, though, and I laugh. "A law?"

Tommy nods. "It's true. Or it was at one point, at least ... I think. I know it's store policy, though. We don't take returns on items like that."

"I thought you were just making that up to fuck with her."

"Well, that's part of it," Tommy says with a wink.

I wonder if there ever really was a law. It sounds logical. There's got to be a major health issue with that kind of thing. Hell, a lot of what's in Adult World, especially on the booth side, is probably a health issue, I would think.

I cringe at the thought and as if on cue, from the back

of the store comes a short, solidly built black man wearing old work clothes and a black, knit cap that at first glance appears to be a bad haircut. He's carrying cleaning supplies and headphones hang around his neck.

"Hey Ellis," Tommy says.

Ellis waves, then glances at me.

"This is Brian. New employee."

Ellis nods hello, puts on his headphones, and proceeds to the booth area to clean.

Suddenly my job at Truman's doesn't look so bad. An occasional bad apple or a spill in aisle three is nothing compared to what Ellis has to clean up.

I could never do what he's doing. Hell, I don't even like to clean up after *myself.*

"Yeesh!" I say to Tommy. "I hope he gets paid well."

"Eh, he doesn't care. He's from Jamaica. Probably just happy to get paid in something other than coconuts."

I laugh ... although it's kind of a mean thing to say. I hope Ellis didn't hear it - or me laughing at it.

But then again, maybe he doesn't care as much as I think he would. The rules seem different in Adult World.

I wish I could say that my first two days at Adult World didn't have an effect on me, but I must admit that seeing all the naked images of women - I ignored the men they were usually with, of course - has made me, well, kind of horny.

So Sunday night, as I hide my Adult World staff shirt in the same drawer where I stashed the Rita Hanson video the night before, I decide to take a look at the video.

And while I look at it in the privacy of my room, I get a little turned on. Not much, though. Mostly during the beginning, before things get, er, up close and personal. Still, it's enough to put me in the mood to want to, well, take matters into my own hands.

It might not even be the video. It could be my own up close and personal contact with Jennifer recently. It could be anything, at any time, frankly.

Hell, at this age, sometimes it's completely out of my control. Sometimes a penis stands at attention all by itself … so attention must be paid.

I wish Jennifer was available to help me. Not that she would do it at this point in our relationship … but I can hope, can't I?

So I'm going along and it's feeling pretty good. I get close to finishing, then right as I'm at *full* attention, my mom knocks on my door and immediately opens it!

Now, my mom knows that I'm eighteen and she's gotta figure there are things that I don't want her to know I do, much less *see* me do, in my bedroom. What would possess her to just open the door without me saying even a simple "Come in" is beyond me.

I scramble to turn off the video and toss away the case. At the same time, I reach for a book to cover my lap, in case it's noticeable what's going on down there.

She looks at me strangely as I settle into my position on the bed like nothing happened.

"How was work?" she says after staring for a few awkward seconds. She can probably sense the air of shame hanging in the room.

"Huh?" I say and try to process the question. It takes me a moment. "Oh, uh, good. Fine." I told her I had to work at Truman's all day.

"You okay?" she asks.

"Yeah. Why?"

"No reason." She looks at me curiously. "Well, dinner's ready."

This *is what you barged into my room for?*

I nod and she leaves.

Now that the mood is shattered like a plate-glass window hit with a hundred-mile-an-hour fastball, I see no point in returning to my mission.

Still, once that launch-sequence has begun, or even been considered, the body seems to want to blast off. So that night I have another sex dream.

After going at it full-throttle for a while, the anonymous woman I'm having sex with changes to Jennifer. There might have been a bit of Rita in there, too, but thankfully she didn't stay very long.

It's kind of cool that Jennifer's made her first appearance. I kind of hope it's a glimpse of the future - my future, with her.

I really want to be with her, especially for my first time. And things would have gone great with her in the dream, had I not been interrupted by the damn beeping sound of my alarm clock!

I suppose I could have finished myself off once I woke up, but it's not the same as it is in dreams. You have to start all over again.

So all day I'm frustrated - so much so that I even look at that morning's magazine and am half-tempted to take it from Mike to, um, *inspire* me later.

But then I'd want to do it during school and I'd end up in a bathroom stall or something, where I'd get caught and from then on my high school life would be over. I'd be forever known as the guy who jacked off at school. I'd get a nickname like "Jack" or "Jerky" or something stupid like that. And it would stick with me forever. It would be like the red *A* in *The Scarlet Letter.* Only with me it would be a *J.*

My sexual frustration is only compounded by Mike's interrogation about what happened with Jennifer on Friday night. I tell him about how she gave me paint brushes and how nice it is and how great she is and all that kind of stuff he couldn't give a rat's ass about - or so he says.

"Paint brushes?" he says. "That's it? Pfft. You at least get anything from Rita?"

"'Rita'?"

"Yeah. At the store. Saturday."

"Oh. No. Ew," I say. It's one thing to have sex with her in a dream - especially when she's part girlfriend, part hot woman of my creation; it's a whole other thing to be with her in real life, especially after I've seen what she's willing to do, or willing to let be done to her, on video.

"Why would I want to do that?" I ask and wonder if he's serious or just talking, as guys do.

"Why *wouldn't* you?"

"I can think of a hundred reasons."

"You're crazy. If I was eighteen, I'd be *all over* those broads that come to the store. Bet they could teach me a few things."

"Or *give* you a few things."

"Nah," Mike says. "They're all clean. They get checked out on a regular basis these days."

"Still ..."

"Well, at least with them you know where you stand. Y'know? You don't have to take 'em out a buncha times to get what you really want."

"Date with Tracy didn't go well, huh?"

"We went to the movies. The *movies.*"

"So? It's a date. You gotta date her, get to know her, first."

"Eh ..." he says with a shrug.

I laugh. "Well, think of it this way, then: You're laying the groundwork."

"I'd rather -"

"Yeah, yeah, yeah. I got it ... you'd rather be 'laying' something else."

Mike smiles. I don't think he's ever even considered the possibility of a relationship with a girl. It's just about sex.

But I'm sure a lot of people think that way these days. It's everywhere - TV, the Internet, magazines, billboards, you name it.

I read in a magazine once that girls are getting their periods earlier now because of all the sexual images they're exposed to, that it somehow triggers it because their minds tell their bodies to be ready for it. How crazy is that?

I imagine the same thing happens for boys. Seeing all that stuff probably tells us to get ready for it earlier, too - especially since it's mostly images of women.

I know Mike saw more than most because of his dad's business, so who knows how it affected him? He's my best friend, but even I don't know when his body became, uh, *ready.*

All I know is he started talking about it all *way* before I did.

Maybe that's normal and I'm not, though. Maybe I'm a late bloomer or something. I don't know.

I have to admit that I feel a lot closer to thinking like Mike after my weekend at Adult World. Even Jennifer seems to notice.

After not seeing her all weekend - and not relieving myself after getting to second base with her on Friday - I'm more forward than normal in our PDA's.

In the lobby after school she keeps saying she has to go to practice, but I don't let her go. I just keep kissing her and getting turned on. I even get wet down there. I feel guilty about it, but, like I said, sometimes it's simply beyond my control.

"What's gotten into you?" she asks.

I smile and pretend that it's only because of the desire for intimacy with her, instead of something more basic. Actually, wanting to be closer to *her* is a big part of the reason I'm so turned on. Really. I'm not just saying that.

"Nothing," I say. "I'm just happy to see you."

She seems to like my answer and lets me kiss her again, but not for long. "C'mon. I gotta get to practice." She makes me stop and leads me back toward where everybody else is.

She probably figures I'll be less aggressive with everybody around. She's right.

"By the way," she says, "my dad wanted me to invite you to dinner Sunday."

"What? Really?"

"Yeah."

"You're kidding, right? I'm probably the last person he wants to see."

"No. That's not true."

"He probably wants to interrogate me or something."

"No … well, maybe a little," Jennifer says with a smile. "I think he just wants to get to know my boyfriend."

It's the first time she's ever called me her boyfriend. I stop to savor the moment.

I'm her boyfriend. She's my girlfriend. We're a couple.

I've never been in a couple before. I like it. I like it so much that I would probably agree to the torture of a Sunday dinner with Jennifer's father if I wasn't scheduled to work at Adult World. "Oh, this Sunday? I can't. I have to work. Sorry."

"How about next week?" she asks.

"Well, I just started, so I probably shouldn't ask off for a little while."

"Haven't you always been at Truman's?"

"Well, I, uh, yeah … but I just started with a new position, so …" I hate to lie to her, but the last thing she probably wants to hear is that I work at a porn store.

"You just don't want to come, do you?"

The double meaning of her sentence strikes me and I try to say, "That's not true at all," without laughing, but I can't quite pull it off.

She looks at me suspiciously. I wonder if she knows what I'm thinking or is just deciding whether I'm lying about not wanting to go to her house for dinner.

"I'll see what I can do," I say.

She accepts this with a smile and starts to walk away for practice. I look around, don't see Mike, and realize that I haven't seen him at all since before school at the baseball field.

"Have you seen Mike?" I say.

Jennifer shakes her head and continues into the locker room. I wish I could follow her, but since I can't, I wait a few more minutes, then head out to the parking lot where Mike parked when we arrived in the morning.

His car is gone. He's left me, high and dry. The buses are now gone, too. And there's no one around to give me a ride.

"I gotta get a car ..." I say to myself as I zip up my winter coat to brace against the cold and begin the long walk home.

On my chilly journey from school, I stop by a 7-Eleven to thaw out for a second and pick up a newspaper to check out prices on used cars before I do a more thorough search on the computer.

I'm still reading the paper when I sit for dinner, mostly because it'll keep me from having to talk to Gary - who once again is at the house mooching a meal off my mom.

"You looking for a car?" he asks me. Either he's totally missed the obvious or just making annoying small talk. "Y'know, my buddy Jeff's sellin' his, if you're interested."

"That's okay," I say. "I'm fine." The last thing I want is Gary's help. He's only doing it to get on my good side, anyway - so he can get on whatever side he wants with my mom.

"It's a great car. A little old, maybe ... but cheap."

"How cheap?" I'm willing to hear him out if it'll save me money. Compromise *is* a part of growing up, isn't it?

"How much you wanna spend?"

"I don't know," I say. "Couple thousand, I guess."

"He's only asking, like, five hundred for it. Something like that."

"Heh. Must be a piece of shit."

My mom hits me on the arm. "Brian ..."

Gary doesn't seem to mind the language, though. My

mom wouldn't, either ... if he wasn't there.

"Hey, it runs," Gary says. "I know that. And he's pretty good with cars, so it can't be in bad shape mechanically. I can give him a call if you want."

"Um, thanks. But I'll be all right." I figure the car's probably not worth the price of letting Gary do me a favor. Plus, maybe Mr. Welch had something in mind when he said he'd help me. Maybe he can get me a deal on a nicer car - like a BMW or something. Well, probably not that, but something good. I'll have to talk to him.

"Well, if you change your mind ..." Gary says and writes down his friend Jeff's phone number on a piece of paper. "Just make sure you tell him you know me."

"That's so nice of you, Gary," my mom says. She stares at me the same way she used to when I was a kid and got a gift from someone.

"Um, yeah, thanks," I say and go back to eating.

After dinner, I call Mike again. I tried him a few times that day, but he never answered. This time he does. I thought maybe something happened to him, like he got sick or something, but from the way he answers, "Yell-o," that's clearly not the case.

"What the hell? Where were you today?"

"Yeah, I ducked out after fifth period," he says.

"Well ya coulda told me ..."

"Sorry, Bro. But I was with Tracy. Gotta invoke the Nookie Clause."

The Nookie Clause is something Mike invented years ago, once he started getting more interested in girls than friendship. It's basically an escape clause for any plans we may have made. All the rules, any consideration, whatever, go out the window if there's a girl involved. And the other person must accept this, no matter what the circumstances. So I accept it, as usual.

"So ... what happened?" I ask.

"A gentleman never tells."

"Since when are you a gentleman?"

"True. I'll tell ya about it tomorrow." I figure nothing happened. Otherwise he would have bragged about it then and there.

"You gonna be there - or should I take the bus?"

"Hey, you could always get your *own* car, y'know ..."

He's right. I need to buy a car - and soon. If not, I will continue to be a victim of Mike's Nookie Clause.

I can't blame him, though. He's seventeen. And it *is* his car.

Also, with my own car I could take Jennifer out whenever I want - not just when my mom's car's available.

So after I get off the phone, I call Mr. Welch to see if he can help me. I get his voicemail.

"Hi, Mr. Welch. Um, I'm looking at cars ... and you said you might be able to help, so I, I thought I'd call you. Not sure what you meant, but ... well, give me a call if you can."

I then figure maybe it's best if he didn't call me. My mom might answer and wonder why he's calling - or worse, he'll mention that I'm working for him at Adult World, which I don't want her to know right now.

"Um, you know what, never mind. Don't call me. I'll try you again later."

I call him at Adult World a little later, but he's not there. I tell Tommy not to bother leaving a message.

I try Mr. Welch again the next day, but he must be really busy because I still don't get him. After some more thought, I decide to find the number of Gary's friend and call him. I tell him I know Gary and he tells me about the car and what he wants for it. I look it up on the Internet to see if it's a good deal and it is. A really good deal, actually. So I go over to look at it the first chance I get.

The old Buick's not nearly as bad as I thought it would be when Gary first told me about it. It's not exactly my style, with mag wheels and flame stickers on the side, but it's clear that the car itself is in good shape. The engine even *looks* clean. And judging from Jeff's appearance - long hair, vintage Chevy T-shirt, torn jeans - and all the mechanical tools and parts in his garage, it's also clear that he knows what he's doing with cars. Plus, I figure he wouldn't screw the son of the woman his friend is, well, *screwing*.

"Yeah, your mom's a real nice lady," Jeff says. "Gary likes her a lot."

I wonder what he means by that and, like most everything else involving my mom and Gary, try to put it out of my mind. I just nod.

"Talks about her all the time."

I nod again and take one last look at the car. I can't see any major flaws, so, despite my reluctance to let Gary do me a favor, I buy the car from Jeff.

But really, when I think about it, it's not like *Gary* did me a favor. It's more like he did his friend a favor. He helped *him* sell his car. The guy made five hundred bucks.

Now, if Gary had *given* me a car ... well, that's a different story.

Still, at the end of the day, it's a pretty good deal for me. The car is worth around four times what I pay for it, which is good. I'll need to strip the flame decals off, of course. I'd like to change the mag wheels, too, but will have to live with them for a while if I want to save money on buying new rims.

I can't wait to tell Mr. Welch about my deal. As a businessman, he'll be proud of me.

Despite the good deal, Mike still makes fun of me for it. "You get a free tattoo with that?" he says when he sees the car for the first time.

"Hey, it runs - and it's paid for," is my answer - and in the end, it's a great one. Not only that, but since it's old, the insurance is much cheaper than Mike pays for his newer BMW. Pride be damned and money be kept in my pocket is all I have to say.

It's amazing how quickly we can get the thing we want when we decide we can't live any longer without it. I suppose that only applies to things, though. People are a different story.

I would love to take Jennifer out with my new car, but since she's still grounded from the night of my birthday, I'm forced to wait until the weekend. While I wait and think about little else except her, I decide to make a pledge not to touch myself anymore. For some reason I think that'll make sex with Jennifer happen faster. Don't ask me where that logic comes from.

I know it'll be hard - pun intended - but I like a challenge. I tell myself that if I lose control at night when I'm sleeping, it's okay - because that's completely out of my control - but I vow that I will not have a hand in it.

It's not easy, because on Saturday I work at Adult World again - and again I'm surrounded by stimulation. It can totally warp your brain if you let it. I try not to and whenever possible, I turn off the videos. There's something about a woman's moan that's impossible to ignore - much harder than just a visual of her naked, having sex. Those are everywhere you look in the store.

Robby doesn't seem to mind it the way I do. And he probably hasn't made the pledge I have.

"What'd you turn it off for?" he asks me.

I shrug. I don't want to tell him why.

"You'll get used to it," he says with a knowing laugh, then turns it back on, "... after a couple months."

I don't think I'll ever get used to it. I'm certainly not used to it by the time I finish work that day and go out with Jennifer, because in the car at the end of the date, I can barely contain myself.

We get really hot and heavy - more than usual. She even lets me put my hand in her pants and rub her. Skin to skin. And she seems to like it. I can tell; she feels wet - like I get, only different.

She stops me after a few minutes, though, like she just wants a brief taste of pleasure. She puts her hand on my crotch and rubs my inflated jeans for a minute or two before reaching beneath them and wrapping her fingers around me - it - and rubs up and down.

It feels really good - especially after my week of self-denial. I hadn't even had a completed sex dream. My subconscious must have more discipline than I thought. But as long as Jennifer does the releasing, self-discipline be damned.

"Don't stop ..." I say.

She smiles, then slows the movement of her hand.

She's clearly teasing me. She knows she has me by the balls - well, not the balls, but close enough - and she's going to use it to her advantage.

"Are you going to come to dinner Sunday?"

"Tomorrow? Uh … I have to … work …" *Oh, God, don't stop*, I'm thinking.

"How about next Sunday?"

"I, I, I have to work then … too."

"But it's Easter. Truman's is closed."

Oh, shit. That's right. Truman's is closed. The owners are very religious.

I fight to send some blood back to my brain so I can explain myself. "Yeah, but … I, um, … I've also been helping Mike's dad. He, uh, owns some real estate and -"

"I'm sure he won't care." She starts to rub me harder and faster, then slows down again and eases her grip.

"I … guess …"

"So you'll come?"

I smile. That's the first thing I want to do at the moment - and she knows it. I wonder if she realizes what she said. She must.

She moves her hand faster, then slows down. I have no other choice but to say yes. I want to finish … badly. "Um, um … okay," is the best I can do.

"Okay, what?" she says as she slows down again.

"I'll … get off … early …" I say and thrust my hip up to get closer, more firmly in her hand - or any part of her I can touch, for that matter.

She smiles - I think; I'm not paying much attention at this point - and let's me shift myself where I need to while she continues to move her hand against me. Within a minute I … *finish* in my pants. I make a hell of a mess, but I don't care, it feels so good. And it's contained, for the most part.

I slide back into my seat as she takes her hand out and stares at me like the victor over the vanquished.

If this is defeat, I'm only too happy to surrender.

Unfortunately, as a result of the loss to Jennifer, I'm forced to be taken prisoner - for at least one Sunday night dinner, anyway. I don't take off from work, but Mr. Welch lets me leave early enough to get to the Kinneys' house for Easter dinner. And I make the mistake of saying this to Mr. Kinney while I'm there - not the Adult World part, of course.

"You had to work? On Easter?" he says. "I hope you were at least able to attend a service."

I know Mr. Kinney's an extremely religious guy, a Deacon at his church or something. I'm not sure what a Deacon is, but it's a title, so that's gotta stand for something.

"Um ... well, to be honest -"

"You weren't being honest up to now?" Mr. Kinney says.

"No. I mean, yes, I was. I just -"

Jennifer interrupts to ease the grilling. "Daddy."

"I'm just teasing you," Mr. Kinney says, all friendly-like. But I know he isn't teasing. "Go on, Brian."

"I was gonna say ... I've never really ... I don't go to church, per se."

"Oh. Where do you go?"

"Sorry?"

Mr. Kinney gives me a judgmental look that I'm getting a little too familiar with. "You said you didn't go to church, *per se*. Where do you go?"

Serves me right for trying to use a big word with the adults. *Per se.* Who the hell says that, anyway? "Well, I, um, my mom was always kinda too busy catching up on the sleep she missed working all week, so ..."

"So your mom isn't a religious person?"

"Um, no. I -"

"Leave him alone, John." This time it's Mrs. Kinney who comes to the rescue. I'm liking her more and more.

"Yeah, Dad," Jennifer adds and looks at me apologetically.

I nod that it's okay. The one-two punch from his wife and daughter silences Mr. Kinney - for a little while, anyway - and I'm able to eat some of the ham dinner in relative peace.

But after dinner it's another story. As Jennifer and her mother clear the table and are more out of the room than in, Mr. Kinney starts up with me again.

"So, Brian," he says, "What are your intentions?"

I figure he's just making small talk and say, "Well, after high school I'm probably going to art school in Philadelphia, so I'm -"

"No. I mean with my daughter," he says. "What are your intentions with Jennifer?"

"Oh," I say and look around. *Where are the ladies when I need them?*

They're in the kitchen, washing dishes.

Damn.

"Um. Well, I, I hadn't really thought about -"

"Sure you have," Mr. Kinney says as he sits back confidently in his chair. "Boys your age can't help it. You're like dogs in heat."

I almost laugh, but quickly realize he's not kidding - not even a little.

The conversation pauses as Mrs. Kinney returns to get

the last of the plates.

"Can I help you with those?" I say.

"Oh, don't be silly," she says with a brush of her hand. "Sit. Talk."

I watch her desperately as she leaves and am forced to turn my attention back to Mr. Kinney.

He leans in close to me and says, "Life's about choices, Brian ... moral choices. On this side you have Godliness; on that side Hedonism. You stay on the right side, you'll be fine. We understand each other?"

I'm thrown by his lecture and can only nod in response.

Mr. Kinney leans back, satisfied that his sermon has been heard. Still, he continues to stare at me to make sure I got it.

I've heard it and I get it, my look says.

Clearly Jennifer never got her dad's lecture - either that or me having dinner at her house meant a *lot* to her - because later that night, after her parents have gone to bed, she takes me down to her basement and unzips my pants again. Only this time, she wants to use more than her hands on me.

"What are you - ?"

She smiles and begins to move down on me. I know what she wants to do and I can't say I don't like it, but still, I feel obliged to remind her that her parents are right upstairs.

"It's okay," she whispers and continues. "They won't come down."

"I don't know ..."

She puts her mouth on me. Third base. Well, *she's* there. Or am I there? Does the giver take the base ... or the receiver?

None of that matters at the moment, though. All I know is it feels *good*.

I'm a little worried about getting caught, but eventually the pleasure takes over and I stop caring. I let her do what she wants.

It doesn't take long for me to lose control, although I struggle to hold it as long as I can. I don't want to go too long, but I also want to enjoy it before I finish. That's half the fun, isn't it?

When I finally feel myself give way, I try to tell her. "I, I, I'm ..." I say and tap her on the shoulder. She doesn't seem to mind and continues to keep her mouth on me.

When it's over, I'm worried about the mess I might have made, but there doesn't seem to be any. I guess she swallowed it - which is kind of surprising, considering she told me she's never done it before.

But I can't quite wrap my brain around that, or anything, at this point. I'm too dizzy. My brain feels like it's swelling in my head, as if all the blood's heading back north at once.

I take a deep breath and collapse. I can barely move my arms or legs. There's no tension left in my body whatsoever. I'm more relaxed than I think I've ever been in my life.

I let out a low moan and look at her smiling face. She's more beautiful than ever.

I then make a feeble attempt to return the favor of pleasure she's given me by using my fingers on her, but she doesn't seem interested. I think she just wants to let me lie back and enjoy the feeling.

So I do.

THIRD

The pleasure of my experience with Jennifer carries me through the rest of the week, both physically and emotionally. It's hard to be unhappy when you take a step forward in a relationship like that. Well, really she did the stepping; I just went along for the ride.

Still, there's a nagging question about her prior experience. I subtly hint at the subject, but nothing she does or says makes me think she's lying about not having done it with anyone else. She even mentions talking about it with one of her more experienced girlfriends before, so I go with that explanation and put it out of my mind.

I keep the whole episode from Mike because I don't want to hear his explanation. In fact, I don't tell anyone. It's between me and Jennifer - and only us. I don't want anyone else to know. I especially don't want anyone at Adult World to know.

But I guess it's impossible to keep male pride completely at bay. I find this out the hard way the following Saturday, when I'm working with Robby and

Mike comes in to Adult World to get his allowance, which he's been doing more on Saturdays now that I'm there.

At one point while Mike's hanging out, Robby stops to watch a video of a woman giving oral sex to a very, uh, *large* man. Mike and I can't help looking, too.

"Damn," Mike says. "She's like a sword-swallower or something. How can she get all that in and not gag?"

I shrug and show absolutely no response for fear I'll give away my secret.

"Chloraseptic," Robby says.

Mike squints at him. "The throat spray?"

"Yup." Robby points inside his mouth. "Numbs the throat."

We all look at the video. The woman's still going at it.

Mike elbows me. "Now *that's* why you wanna do it with someone like her. Would Jenny do that?"

Before I can think, I say, "Why do you assume she hasn't?" I probably would have said the same thing had she not done it, just to mess with him, but I feel doubly bad for saying it since she has.

Mike laughs. "Yeah, sure. I know you're still a bat boy."

I make a face like he caught me in a lie and that thankfully seems to put an end to the subject ... until Robby pipes in.

"'Jenny'? Is that your girl, Brian?"

I nod.

"How old is she?"

"Old enough," Mike says.

"Seventeen."

Robby squints and inhales like he's reverse-whistling. "Ooooh. And she's ..." He makes a tongue-in-cheek sign for oral sex.

I fight a reaction, but can't help smiling. So I turn away to hide it.

"C'mon," he prods. "You can tell me. She sharpen your pencil yet? She pop your lolli? Play your fife and drums?"

I laugh.

"Oh, yeah," Robby says. "Now we're talkin' ..."

Mike looks at me as I continue to hide my expression.

It must show on my face somehow, though, because Mike's eyes widen. "Holy shit! She *did*."

"I didn't say that."

"But you didn't *not* say it," Robby says.

Mike shakes his head at me. "He's always been terrible at hiding the truth." In a Popeye voice he adds, "Well, blow me down!"

I shake my head, turn away, and focus on work. I've already given away too much.

"So ... did she ... y'know ... glug, glug?" Robby says.

I stop and glare at him. "That's crossing the line."

"There are no lines in here," he says. "C'mon. She take it down the drain or not?"

Mike joins in the prodding. "Yeah, Popeye. Make with the details. She lick your Twinkie clean or get hit by a pitch?"

"You kiss your mother with that mouth?" I say.

"No, I kiss yours with it ..."

Thankfully the subject is dropped when Mr. Welch enters and sees Mike. "What are you doing here?"

All the confidence Mike had during the interrogation is gone in an instant. "Nothing. Just stopped in to see you and -"

"How long have you been in the store?"

"I just got here."

Mr. Welch turns to me. "How long's he been here,

Brian?"

"Um, not long," I say. "Not long at all."

Mr. Welch stares at me a few seconds longer. He must believe my lie, because his face softens. "Well, don't stay long," he says to Mike. "I don't want to get shut down."

Mike nods humbly.

"Mr. Welch," I say, "I bought a car."

"You did? Already? Why didn't you tell me? I told you I'd hook you up."

I'm still not sure what he means. "I know. But I know you're busy ... and it was a pretty good deal."

"What'd you get?"

"A Buick. It's outside. Did you see it?"

"That's yours?"

I nod.

"A Buick? No, no. Ya gotta get a Beemer ... a Mercedes ... Audi ... something like that ... something to get you the girls. Rule Number One: It's about the girls." He winks.

"Well, I can't really afford any of those. And this was only five hundred bucks, so -"

"Five hundred? That's it?" He seems impressed.

"Yeah. And it's in really good shape. I looked it up. Probably worth like four times what I paid, so -"

"That *is* pretty good. Good for you, my boy. Money's always better than girls." He puts his hand on my shoulder and winks again. I smile and nod in agreement.

He takes out his wallet and hands me twenty dollars. "Here. For gas." He smiles at me, then says, "Speaking of money ..." and looks at Robby. He tilts his head toward the back and Robby follows him.

I turn to Mike and smile proudly at his dad's approval, but he doesn't seem to care. He shakes his head and returns to interrogation mode. "So now that you have wheels, when're you gonna ..." He punches his fist in his palm.

"What?" I say. "Get into a fist-fight?"

Mike smirks. "No. With Jenny. Come home. Run the gamut. Plow the field. Bang. Boff. Fungo."

"That's not really up to me, is it?"

"Sure it is. I mean, hell, if she's already going down on you ..."

"If," I make a point of saying.

"Whatever."

"It's a different thing for a girl." And it is, what with pregnancy and the loss of virginity and all. I don't think guys worry about it as much - at least not the virginity part, anyway.

"God, you're such a sissy-la-la."

I laugh off the dig as Mr. Welch returns with Robby and heads to the door. "C'mon, Mike. Out."

Mike sighs, follows his father, then stops and looks back at me. "Seriously, Bro," he says and punches his fist in his palm again before leaving.

I turn to Robby to see his reaction to Mike, but he doesn't seem to have one. He's looking up at the television. "Whoa! Thar he blows!"

I look up at the television just in time, unfortunately, to see the visual evidence of the end of the oral sex act. It's pretty disgusting to watch it happen to someone else.

Even though I work a lot now and usually don't care one way or the other about school sporting events, I've started to go to as many as I can just to watch Jennifer cheer. It's really cute - and sometimes very sexy. They do a lot of bumping and grinding, sometimes with each other - right there in front of all the families that have come to see their kids compete! And nobody complains. It's amazing what we consider normal today.

Only recently has Jennifer started to acknowledge me in the stands while she cheers, which, I must say, gives me a thrill - especially when other people notice that she's looking at me.

At one point during a Saturday night basketball game a few weeks - and a few physical encounters - after the dinner at her house, she looks at me right in the middle of a routine and I think she even licks her lips.

It *so* turns me on!

I'm sitting with Mike and I guess he notices, because he makes a face. I think he's sort of jealous - whether of her or me, I can't tell. She has taken up a lot of my time and since I have my own car now, I haven't seen him much. And he hasn't seen any more of Tracy Bowman. Like all the others, she didn't last long.

After the game, we wait in the lobby - me for Jennifer, him for me - before proceeding to the usual after-game dance. As Jennifer comes out of the gym, I see her say something to Rick Schmidt. He's one of the basketball players. Had a good game, too ... the bastard.

Mike takes note of their conversation - again. He never misses these things. "You think she ever ... with him?" he asks me and sticks his tongue in his cheek.

"Stop that," I say and stand in front of him in case Jennifer looks our way and sees him do it. "I know she didn't."

"How do you know?"

"She told me. I'm her first."

"And, of course, you believed her."

"Yeah. Why wouldn't I?"

Mike shakes his head at me. "Boy, are you naive. You think Joe Bohunk over there's gonna hang around for long without some action?"

The thought crosses my mind, but again, I don't even want to think about it.

Of course Mike keeps pushing it. "How long they go out?"

"I dunno, Mike. Coupla months, maybe. So what?"

"And how far have you gotten in just a coupla weeks?"

He does have a point. But she really likes me and has said so. And she knows I like her ... and only her. "That's different," I say, not sure what else I can say.

Mike laughs that condescending laugh of his, which is, thankfully, interrupted by the ring of his phone. He answers it. "Hey, Dad. What's going on? Yeah, he's here. Why? Alright, alright."

Mike looks irritated as he hands me the phone. "My dad. Wants to talk to you."

I'm still watching Jennifer. She's waved goodbye in a friendly way to Rick and is headed toward me, so I feel a lot better about the idea of me being the only person she's ever gone down on.

I answer the call from Mr. Welch, nod hello to Jennifer, then make an apologetic face and turn away so she can't hear Mr. Welch on the phone. He asks me if I can work an overnight.

"Um, tonight?"

"Yeah. Robby's tied up doing something else."

"Oh. Well ..." I say and think about how I don't really want to work.

But he's pretty insistent. "Don't let me down," he says. "I'm counting on you. You're the only one." That kind of thing. So, of course, I have no other choice.

And, as always, there's the money. He throws in an

extra twenty dollars.

"Yeah, I guess I can," I say, all the while thinking, *Shit. Now what do I tell Jennifer?*

I don't know why I have such a hard time saying no - especially to adults. Maybe I like to think I'm being responsible. But I don't know.

Once Mr. Welch has me committed, he's ready to jump off the phone.

"Okay," I say. "You want to talk to Mike again?"

He says no and hangs up.

I hand the phone to Mike and he lifts it to his ear. "Dad?"

"He hung up."

"Oh." Mike makes a disappointed face.

I remember when he was a kid and Mr. Welch wasn't around a lot. I know it used to bother him and can see how even a tiny dismissal like this still gets to him.

"He, uh, said he'd talk to you later," I say to soothe the sting of it. "He sounded busy."

Mike nods and seems to feel a little better.

I smile and turn to Jennifer, who's now looking at me with disappointment. She no doubt got the gist of my phone conversation.

"I'm sorry. It's kind of an emergency. I, uh, I gotta go help Mike's dad ... y'know, the real estate stuff ..." I glance at Mike to make sure he doesn't - and won't - give away the truth.

Jennifer looks disappointed. "On a Saturday night?"

"Yeah, I know. I'm so sorry. I'll totally make it up to you. I promise." I smile at her.

"How'm I gonna get home?" she says.

"Oh. Damn. I didn't think about that." I don't know what I was thinking.

Mike steps in. "Relax, Bro. I can give her a lift."

"That's okay," Jennifer says. "I'll find a ride."

"It's no big deal," Mike says.

I look at him, then Jennifer, while I try to come up with another option. Rick's still in the lobby and the idea that maybe she'll get a ride from him crosses my mind.

Dammit! If only I hadn't gotten on the phone ...

"I could run you home now," I say.

"Everybody's going to the dance ..."

"Oh. Right."

Double Dammit!

"She'll be fine," Mike says, then turns to her for further reassurance. "You'll be fine. Seriously."

I look at Mike to make sure he hasn't been drinking. He looks clean, but I still check to make sure when Jennifer is distracted by a friend passing by.

"You're not drinking tonight, right?" I whisper.

He raises his hand like he's taking the witness stand and shakes his head, so I feel confident of Jennifer's safety.

She turns back from her friend and I wait for her to accept the arrangement. "Okay?"

She doesn't seem happy about it, but nods anyway.

"I'm really sorry," I say. "I'll call you tomorrow." I kiss her and turn to Mike. "Thanks, Buddy. Appreciate it."

"No problem, Bro."

I hope Mike doesn't get distracted by someone like Tracy again and force Jennifer to find a ride from someone else.

Before I leave, I tell Jennifer and Mike, "Call me if there's any problem. I'll come get you."

I don't know how I will - or how she can even reach me - but I'll figure something out.

At least Mike knows where I'll be. He can call me.

The overnight shift at Adult World is like watching oil paint dry on a canvas. For the first two hours, there are only four customers, so I occupy myself by sketching.

I find that I'm drawing a lot of female nude forms these days. It's something a lot of artists do and I should be doing it; I only wish my reason was more artistic and not just that it's on my mind a lot. Still, some of the sketches are pretty good. I guess at the end of the day passion is passion, no matter what form it takes.

At one point, a few hours into my shift, Ellis comes in to clean. He barely acknowledges my presence. In fact, the first words I think he ever says to me are when he comes out and tells me, in his thick, Jamaican accent, "There's a boot down back dare, Brian."

I'm surprised he even knows my name.

"Oh, uh, okay," I say. "Is it cleaned?"

I don't know why it matters. Maybe he wants me to go back and see if I can fix the booth myself or something. Normally I love to solve problems, but after a moment of thought, I figure this one's probably better left to someone else. Mr. Welch told me not to worry about the booths, anyway, so I have a pass.

Ellis looks at me like I'm a moron. "'Is it clean?' What ya think I been doin'?"

"Well, I try *not* to think about it," I say with a sympathetic smile.

He softens. "You and me, bote. Wouldn't do it wit-out da rubber." He snaps his rubber glove and adds, "Like most tings," with a wink and a smile.

We both laugh, then Ellis' face turns serious and I turn to see Mr. Welch enter the store a little wobbly, like Mike gets when he's drunk. His face is sterner, though.

"Get to work, you two!" he says. "I'm not paying you to stand around!" He laughs and waves at us to show he's only kidding, then walks to the register and opens it.

"There's a booth down in the back," I say. "I'm gonna make a sign."

Mr. Welch nods like he doesn't care - at least not at the moment - and takes money out of the register. As he does, a very pretty black girl, maybe in her mid-twenties, thin, with angular facial features like a model might have, comes through the front door.

Mr. Welch looks up. "Angela, what are ya doin'? I told you to wait in the car."

"I need to use the bathroom," she says. Her voice is sweet and pleasant. Her presence alone brightens the surroundings. She seems in direct contrast to Mr. Welch and I wonder what she's doing with him.

"Hold it in," he says to her. "I'll only be a minute."

I nod hello to Angela and she returns it with a smile.

"This is Brian ... and Ellis," Mr. Welch says. "'Hardest working men in show-business.' Gonna lose Brian to school come the fall, though. Art school. Right, Brian?"

I nod, unsure where he's going with this.

"You believe that? I try to tell him it's a waste of money. Art is dead. Better off using that cash to start a business. Look at me. I never went to school and I make more than most guys I know who did. Not much you can do with an art degree. Just ask Tommy. He went to film school - Temple ... in Philadelphia - while he worked here. I tell him, 'You want to be in the film business? *This* is the film business.'" He stares at me and smiles a drunken smile. "Anyway ... you're a good kid, Brian. Maybe you'll change your mind."

I say nothing. I won't change my mind - I don't think.

It all comes down to the money, though. I hate that.

Mr. Welch rubs my head and turns to Angela. "Ready?"

She nods.

"All right, Brian, see ya in the morning. I'll be in early. I wanna talk to you about something."

I nod and he escorts Angela out the door. Ellis watches them leave, shakes his head, turns to me with a knowing look - just what he knows I can't quite tell - and goes back to work.

Mr. Welch's drunkenness makes me again think of Mike and whether he got Jennifer home okay. I thought he would have called to let me know, but he hasn't yet.

It's too late to call Jennifer, so I call Mike from the store phone. I get his voicemail.

"Hey Man, just calling to see if it went okay. Give me a call ..."

As I hang up, a man enters the store, avoids my gaze, and heads straight back to the booth area. Once again I'm left with nothing to do. I've done enough sketching and look around for something else to do to pass the time.

As I stare out at the store and, in particular, the way it's laid out, I think about Truman's. I remember reading in one of the grocer's magazines in the break room that the layout of the store is one of the most important sales tools in the grocery business. Like, for instance, grocers place the aisles in a way that keeps people lingering in the store longer, so they'll buy more. They also put the staples - meat, dairy, etc. - toward the back, so customers have to go through the rest of the store to get there. And they put candy and other items aimed at children on lower shelves, so kids can see - and grab - them. That kind of thing.

I consider how the same thing - only on a much

smaller scale, of course - might work for Adult World and set about rearranging the aisles and a few of the shelves to do the same thing. I do a bunch of simple things like move the top selling videos to the back and turn the aisles on angles that will slow shoppers down in the store.

The process takes me a few hours, but I don't mind. It makes the time go faster.

The next morning, when Tommy arrives for work, he doesn't immediately notice the change in the layout.

"How was your first overnight?" he asks as he pulls off his coat sleepily and takes his place at the register.

"Dead."

He looks out at the store and squints. "What'd you do in here? Did you do that?"

I shrug yes. "I was bored. Did a little organizing."

"Easy, there, cowboy. What're you trying to do, make me look bad?"

"No, no. I just -" I start to say, but stop as Mr. Welch enters. He looks a little hung over, but is smiling.

"Hey, Boss," Tommy says. "What're you so happy - ? Ah … End of the month, eh?"

Mr. Welch ignores the comment, stops, and looks. "What the hell'd you do to my store?" He doesn't seem happy about the changes.

"I, uh, had some downtime," I say, "and I, uh, was looking at the way the store was laid out. I figured, y'know, if you moved these racks like this, you could change the way people move through it. A little slower. Y'know, like they do at the grocery store, so they buy more. I probably should have asked you, but -"

"Did it work?"

"Um, I don't know. I mean, there were only like five or six people that came in since I did it, but they spent a lot, so ..."

Mr. Welch looks around, then slowly begins to nod. He looks at me, smiles, and turns to Tommy. "See what I was tellin' ya, Tommy? Initiative."

Tommy shoots me a sharp look, as if to say, *"kiss-ass."*

"Actually, Tommy and I talked about it the other day," I say and look at Tommy for him to go along with me. "I just happened to have the time ..."

Mr. Welch turns to Tommy to see if it's true. Tommy nods in agreement.

Mr. Welch looks back at me and I nod for additional confirmation. "Oh. Well, good work ... both of you." He takes a glance in the register, checks the rest of the store, as if to make sure everything's okay, then turns to me. "Brian, what're you doing today?"

"Um, working ... for you ... here."

"Good. Come with me. I want to talk to you. Tommy, you okay without him for a little while?"

Tommy nods and stares at me as I gather my things. I look back, puzzled about what Mr. Welch could want. Tommy shrugs.

Mr. Welch takes me for a ride through the middle of town, where things are more rundown than they are everywhere else, and points to several row homes he owns. So *technically* I wasn't lying to Jennifer about the whole real estate thing, which I feel good about.

"That's mine," he says. "That too. And that. I've been

buying these up ever since the market crashed. One day I'll own this whole street." He nods proudly and looks at me. "Rule Number One: It's all about ownership in this world, Brian, my boy. Ownership. Got it?"

I nod.

"I know you're going to be an artist and all, but you gotta think about your future. You keep making smart business decisions, you won't have to be one of those guys who goes from dreamer to bum. Know what I mean?"

I nod again, even though I'm not sure what he's trying to say.

"You have a lot of potential, Brian. A lot. And a good head for business. Better than Mike - but don't tell him I said that." He winks. "You could do really well for yourself ... for your family. I know you have a girlfriend and all ..."

"Yeah, but I'm not thinking about that stuff yet. I'm still -"

"No one does. But before you know it ..." he says and makes a face that says to me, *You never know what life's gonna throw at you.*

I hadn't really considered it - marriage, family, all that - before, but maybe he's right. Who knows what could happen? Then there's Jennifer. She could be it ... the One. It's all so hard to see.

"You'll figure it out," he says with a confident smile.

"I hope so."

"You will." He winks.

After the brief tour, which is no doubt to get me in the right frame of mind for what he wants to talk to me about, Mr. Welch takes me to Indian Valley Country Club for breakfast - which is good, because after working all night, I'm starving.

I've never been to Indian Valley before and am a bit underdressed for the experience, but thankfully, since I was called in last night, I'm not wearing my Adult World shirt. So I look okay.

"Nice place, huh?" Mr. Welch says as a waiter sets a plate of steak and eggs in front of him.

"Yeah."

"You like it?"

I nod and dig into my chocolate chip pancakes.

"How 'bout I add you to my family membership. Would you like that?"

"Um, you don't have to do that."

"What'd I say Rule Number One was?"

I try to think of which rule number one he's talking about. There've been so many. I figure it's probably the one about always taking whatever people offer you and I say so.

"Right," he says with a wink and finger-gun point at me.

"Won't they, y'know, ask to see proof or something?"

"Don't worry about it. One of the salesmen rents a place from me. I'll get him to print you up a card. Just don't dime him out if you get caught. I know you won't, though. You're a smart kid. Always have been." He winks at me again.

I have to admit, I kind of like the attention. And in this setting I feel more grown-up.

"In fact," Mr. Welch continues, "that's what I want to talk to you about." He takes a bite of his steak, wipes his mouth with his napkin, and after a beat, says, "I want you to be my weekend manager."

I'm surprised.

"Now, I know it's more responsibility, but I have faith in you. I know you can handle it."

I know I can handle it, too. That's not what I'm worried about. What I'm worried about is the fact that he's asking *me*. "What about Robby? Isn't he next in line?"

"Don't worry about Robby. You're my boy on this one, Brian. Like I said ... a head for business." He winks.

"I don't know. I mean, I appreciate the offer and all. I just ... with school and my other job ..."

"Eh, you can quit that job," Mr. Welch says with a dismissive wave of his hand. "I'll more than make up the difference."

I'm not sure what he means by that, but again I assume he means money. And I gotta admit, it's pretty tempting. I do like how good it feels to work for him and how he treats me.

"I'll even throw in an extra thousand bucks if you work through the summer," he says. "Consider it a signing bonus. For college, if you decide to go."

"Oh, I'm go -"

"Plus, I'll need to give you a phone, so I can reach you when I need to."

He can probably see the excitement grow on my face. This is sounding better by the minute. "When would you want me to start?"

"Immediately."

"Well, I don't really want to cause any problems at Truman's. I'd have to give them notice or something."

"I admire your loyalty, but c'mon, Brian, my boy, move up to the big leagues. Reach your potential. Do you intend to work at a grocery store the rest of your life? Trust me; that's a bridge you can burn. By the way, here's your pay for the last coupla weeks."

To put the final period at the end of his already overwhelming argument, he hands me an envelope with all my pay in it - in *cash*.

"That way the government won't take most of it," he says with a sly smile. I do a quick check of the money. It's all there. It's a lot compared to what I'd make at Truman's for the same hours. And it's tax-free.

I know he writes checks to everybody else. I figure he wants to take care of me. I *am* sort of like a son … well, a stepson, anyway.

"So whaddya say?"

There's nothing else to say. I'd be a fool to turn him down, especially with college looming.

After my Adult World shift and before working at Truman's that night, I call Jennifer from the payphone outside the grocery store. I wanted to call earlier, but couldn't from Adult World or she'd see where I was by the phone number.

I suppose I could have blocked it, but I couldn't take the chance that it wouldn't work.

She doesn't answer, so I leave a message.

"Hey, it's me. I'm sorry I'm just calling now. I've been crazy busy. I'll tell you about it later. I just wanted to make sure everything worked out okay last night. I'm sure it did, but … anyway … Sorry about that. I made a lot of money, though, so … I'm going to work at Truman's right now. Working 'til ten. Anyway … I'm thinking of you. I guess I'll talk to you later … I hope. Lemme know."

I worry that Jennifer's mad at me for ditching her and I can't blame her. But what else could I do? Say no?

I guess I could have, but figure Mr. Welch offered me

the manager job based on the fact that I was willing to show up last minute like that. And I'm gonna need the money.

Plus, from now on I'll have a cell phone, which is pretty cool. I'll be able to call Jennifer whenever I need to.

Although ... now Mr. Welch'll be able to get a hold of me when I'm not with Mike. So what happened on Saturday night may happen again at some point.

I make a vow that I will never answer the phone if Mr. Welch calls while I'm with Jennifer. And I'll make sure to tell her this. It should help smooth things over.

For all I know, she may not even be bothered. Maybe I'm just over-thinking it. I hope that's the case.

I go into Truman's and later that night, after working three straight shifts - the two at Adult World, this one at Truman's - and feeling totally exhausted, I duck my head into Dave's office.

"Can I, uh, talk to you a second?"

"Sure, Brian." He waves me in. "What's up?"

"Um, well, I, uh, I kinda have to give you ... well, I can't really give you notice, but is it a problem if I stopped working here?"

"Whatsamatter? There something wrong? You okay?"

"No. Uh, I mean, yeah, I'm okay. I just, I got another job. I hope it isn't a problem."

"No. It's not a problem. I mean, I hate to lose you, but I'm glad to hear you got a better job. Where're you gonna be working?"

"Um ... for my friend's dad. He has a, uh, real estate business."

"Great," he says. "Not a bad business to learn. Not a bad business at all."

"Um, yeah. I guess."

"Only for the summer, though, right?" Dave says with a look of concern. "You're still gone in August."

"Oh, yeah. I'm still going ... as long as I can afford it, that is. This should help."

"Good," he says happily and points to the painting I made for him as a Christmas gift last year. "'Cause I want that to be worth a lot of money some day."

It's not the best thing I ever painted; just an apple on a wooden table, a glimmer of light reflected off it. Kind of Impressionistic, with a really thick application of deep red paint. *Impasto*, they call it - the application, not the red.

The work is better than I remember, now that I look at it again.

"That's my retirement fund," he says.

"I hope so," I say, going along with the over-optimism. *If only ...*

We talk some more about how long I've worked at the store and how I've grown since I started, that kind of thing.

When he walks me to the door, he says, "You're a good man, Brian. You ever need a recommendation - or anything - you come to me. Okay?"

It's a nice thing to say, but I almost wish he hadn't said it. It makes me feel bad that I'm leaving so quickly.

But, again, I need to think about the money. I need to think about my future.

As the automatic door opens for me, I pause and look back before leaving the store for the last time as an employee. It's a little frightening, but I think it's the right thing to do. I've outgrown Truman's.

I haven't talked to either Mike or Jennifer since after the basketball game Saturday night, so by the time I sleepwalk my way into my house late Sunday night, I still don't know if he got her home without any trouble. I assume he did; otherwise, I probably would have heard from someone.

There aren't any messages from her on the home answering machine - just one left by Gary earlier in the day that my mom didn't erase. He actually calls her "babe" in it, which cracks me up. So cheesy.

It's too late to get in touch with Jennifer, and even if it wasn't, I doubt I'd call her, anyway. I'm a little bothered that she hasn't at least checked in with me to let me know everything's okay.

Maybe I should be more concerned about her, but am just too exhausted to worry about much of anything at this point. So it'll all have to wait until tomorrow.

Monday morning I hit the snooze button on my alarm clock three times to squeeze every last minute of sleep I can from the morning. As a result, I'm almost late for school, so I don't have a chance to see Mike at the baseball field and get some answers about Saturday.

I also don't have a lot of time to spend with Jennifer at her locker before homeroom. But in the time I do have I apologize as much as I can and ask her if everything was okay on Saturday.

"It was fine," she says. There's a weird tone in her "fine," though, like she doesn't want to talk about it.

"I'm so sorry." She nods and says nothing. "Oh, and guess what? I'm gettin' a cell phone from Mr. Welch ... for work. So now you can call me or text me or whatever, whenever you want." I smile big, trying to change the mood.

She looks at me blankly.

"But I promise I won't answer work calls when I'm with you," I say and raise my hand like a Boy Scout making a pledge.

She looks like she wants to smile, but fights it.

"Again, I'm so sorry. It'll never happen again. I swear. On a stack of Bibles."

"You don't have to do that."

"No, seriously. Find me a stack of Bibles," I say and look around at some of the other kids in the hallway. "Is there a stack of Bibles around here anywhere?"

She laughs at my silliness. "Stop it."

I stare in her eyes and say, "I really am sorry, y'know."

The relentless apologies must finally work because she smiles, nods, and says, "I know. You had to work. It's okay."

She says nothing else on the subject as we make small talk before the bell rings for homeroom. I continue to think she's not telling me something, but don't pursue it further. I'm just happy she's still talking to me. She even gives me a kiss before she leaves. So whatever was bothering her over the weekend - if anything even was - can't be all that bad.

Still, when I catch up with Mike in the hallway later in the day, I ask, "So ... what happened Saturday?"

"What do you mean?"

"With Jennifer."

"Oh. Nothing. Why?"

"You never called me back to tell me what happened.

You gave her a ride home, right?"

"Yeah," he says. "No big deal."

"Okay. She just ... she sounded weird when I talked to her."

Mike shrugs.

"I thought maybe something happened," I say. "Like, at the dance. Maybe something with Rick Schmidt ... something like that."

"I didn't see anything."

"You didn't tell her what I was doing, did you?"

"No."

"You sure? I mean, maybe you didn't say it on purpose, but, y'know while you were in the car ..."

"No. I didn't tell her where you were," Mike snaps at me.

I don't know why he gets upset. Maybe he doesn't like that I accused him of diming me out. Either that or he's just pissed I made him drive my girlfriend home.

But he seemed fine with it on Saturday.

Maybe the simple fact that I work at his dad's store has gotten to him.

Whatever it is, I say, "I'm sorry," to cover all bases.

He brushes the subject off with a nod and seems to forget all about whatever was bothering him.

I consider that maybe I'm just too sensitive about stuff like this and that it's not a big deal. "Well, she's probably just a little bothered I left," I say.

He nods.

"I'll make it up to her this weekend."

"Don't forget Saturday," he says.

"What's Saturday?"

He stares at me in disbelief and it takes me a second to scan through my mental calendar before I remember.

"Oh, yeah. Right. I know." Mike's eighteenth birthday

is on Saturday. He's planned the celebration for months - a party at his dad's house. Mr. Welch is supposedly even going to send some strippers over for him.

I'm glad it's going to be at his dad's house and not his mom's. I want the party to happen as far away from my house as possible. I'd hate for my mom to drive by, see all the goings-on, and find out I'm a part of whatever crazy thing Mike has cooked up.

When I see Jennifer at the end of the school day, I'm extremely nice to further make up for the blow-off at the game. I ask if she wants to get together later and she says, "I'd love to, but I have a report due tomorrow."

"Oh. Well, what's it on?"

"I have to analyze a poem for English."

"What's the poem?"

"'Past, Present, and Future' by Emily Bronte."

"I can help you with that."

"You know it?"

"No," I say with a smile. It doesn't matter what the poem is; I'll still help her.

She laughs and shakes her head at me in her way that tells me I'm being cute. "I would love that, but I need to do it and if you're there ..."

"I promise I won't distract you."

"Yeah, but I might want to distract you," she says with a suggestive smile that makes me completely forget what I was worried about regarding leaving her on Saturday. "I'm gonna have dinner with my family and all, so ..."

I understand and don't press the issue. "Can I at least give you a ride home?"

"I have practice."

"I know," I say. "I can wait."

"You don't have to. Kim can give me a ride."

"I know I don't have to. I want to."

"What are you going to do for two hours?"

I shrug. "I can go home and come back."

"No. You don't have to -"

"Or I can just hang out here and watch you practice."

"You really wanna do that for two hours?"

I nod. "Would you really love to see me later ... if it wasn't for your paper?"

She smiles. "Yes."

"Then I'll wait."

She kisses me passionately for a good - great, actually - thirty seconds, which of course makes me even more willing to wait as long as it takes.

So I do.

As Jennifer and the other cheerleaders gather for practice, I find a seat at the top of the bleachers, take out my sketchbook and pencils, and survey the gymnasium.

Besides the cheerleaders rehearsing their routines, in another section there's the marching band and majorettes running their drills, complete with spinning flags and wooden rifles. They're not nearly as sexy as the cheerleaders, but impressive in their own way because of the large number of people that are synchronized, each person doing complicated moves and spins, all the while staying in regimented formation.

The marchers aren't perfect, though, because while I'm looking, one of the majorettes drops her rifle and there's a loud crack as it hits the floor. It must have been tossed high and hit one of the band's saxophone players on the way down, because several people run over to make sure he or she is okay.

I look closer and see that the victim is none other than my inadvertent birthday party host, Karen Lutz. She nods to let everyone know she's okay, excuses herself, and heads to the locker room with her hand pressed on her head.

On her way, she walks right in front of me. I nod hello, but as usual since the night of the party, she doesn't acknowledge my presence - even though I know she sees me.

I think she's still pissed at Mike for volunteering her house as a gathering place, and since he's my friend, I get some of the blame for what happened after we left.

Apparently, her parents came home early the next day and lost their minds when they saw that she had a party. It was obvious from the beer cans on the front lawn, the moved furniture, the giant hole in the living room wall, and, worst of all, the damage done to Mr. Lutz's precious hat collection. Those weren't cheap hats people tossed around and jammed on their sweaty heads.

I feel guilty for partaking in it all, but still, when I think about it, I can't help laughing. It's pretty funny, everybody in those hats. And it's no doubt the most action the hats'll ever see.

Maybe the most Karen'll ever see, too. Sure, she got grounded for two weeks, but now she has a story to tell for the rest of her life. It'll probably even be one she tells with a laugh later on or at high school reunions when people remind her of how great her party was that night. In fact, already it's become legendary at school.

So despite the trouble it caused with her parents, the

whole episode's given Karen a certain level of street cred she never had before, which is a good thing in the world of high school.

And since that's the case, she really shouldn't be all that mad at Mike. And definitely not at me. But if that's the way she feels, she's entitled. It's her life.

Once the marching band begins moving again, I focus my attention on the cheerleaders and do some rough sketches of what I see below.

Halfway through my first drawing of the short-skirted girls doing high kicks in a line, I get the notion to make a series that I can eventually convert into pastel works in the style of Edgar Degas and his ballet portraits - only with cheerleaders. I'm totally excited by the idea and sketch furiously, flipping to a new page and hopping to another spot on the bleachers for a different perspective after each completed image.

In my excitement, I don't even notice the two hours fly by, and before I know it, Jennifer's calling to me from the gym floor.

I take a moment to finish a last sketch and by the time I look up she's bouncing from bench to bench up to me.

I slam the sketchbook closed.

"What are you doing?" she asks.

"Just drawing."

"Can I see?"

"They're not really done. Just rough sketches."

"That's okay."

"Let me work on them some more. Then I'll show you."

She looks disappointed, but accepts it. She knows I'm sensitive about my work and only show people - even her - some of it.

It's something I know I'll have to get over eventually,

but for now, having not studied in college yet, I keep it pretty close to the vest.

"You promise?" she asks.

"Yes."

I actually feel pretty good about the sketches I did and think they'll look great when I make the more elaborate pastel works. Getting to spend some time with Jennifer her now is just icing on the cake of what has turned out to be a great day.

I put my arm around her and we hop in lockstep down the bleachers and out to my car.

As I drive her home she nuzzles closer and rests her head on my shoulder.

I'm so happy.

FOURTH

Every free moment I have during the week before Mike's party I spend making pastels of the pencil sketches I did of the cheerleaders. They turn out really well, I think. I take a little liberty and light the cheerleaders from below, like the footlights of Degas' images, and it gives them a sexier quality than the overhead halogen lights of the gymnasium do.

I know I should be doing schoolwork all week instead, but chalk my laziness up to a bad case of Senioritis.

I've always been that way with schoolwork, though, especially once I started really getting into painting and drawing.

Still, I manage to get pretty good grades - good enough to get me into the University of Arts, anyway. Hopefully good enough to get me a scholarship, too.

In between school, my artwork, and work at Adult World, I squeeze in as much Jennifer time as I can. And the more I see her, the more I *want* to see her.

I feel strong and positive about not only the relationship, but myself, which is unusual for me.

Not that I'm a negative person. Just not always the bubbliest in the room. I think that comes with the whole "tortured artist" thing, although which came first, the mood or the art, is hard to tell.

Regardless, this change of pace feels good and shows me that I don't have to be miserable to make good art - or what *I* think is good, anyway.

Unfortunately, I have to work on Friday night, so I won't get to go out with Jennifer until Sunday, because of Mike's birthday party.

From the way he talks about it all week, you'd think Saturday night was going to be the greatest night of his life.

"It's gonna be so awesome," he says at one point while we're sitting at the baseball field before school. "I think my dad's gonna get Nikki Summers to come over after her appearance at the store. Check her out."

He shows me a photo of three women having sex.

"Which one's her?"

He points to a blonde on the left, who's wearing a strap-on and doing it doggy-style with the woman in the center.

I nod and pretend to be impressed. She's actually not too bad looking, although it's hard to tell through the contorted expression of what I assume is supposed to be pleasure on her face.

"Man, I can't wait." Mike takes another look at the photograph, squints, and sucks air in through his teeth with aching anticipation.

I think in his head he somehow imagines he'll be the one giving her that look of pleasure come Saturday night.

We'll see.

The expression on Nikki's face in Mike's photo is a far cry from the blank look she has while signing prints of a tamer photo for customers at Adult World on Saturday.

Unlike Rita's, Nikki's appearance fills the store with men and women, both equally interested in seeing the actress in the flesh. I'm not sure why at first. She does seem sexier, a little younger, maybe less "worn" than Rita. She's still got a lot of miles on her, though, as Robby notes.

When Mike enters the store, he looks her up and down, then mouths, "Awesome," as he approaches the counter, where I'm working with Tommy, Robby, and Charlie.

"Your dad's not here, Spanky," Tommy says to Mike.

"So?" Mike says.

"So, you probably shouldn't be in here."

"It's okay," I say. "He's legal as of Thursday."

"That's right. I'm outta the minors. And I wanna check out what I'm getting into later." Mike tilts his head toward Nikki and clicks his cheek.

"Oh, I'm sure she'll love that," Tommy says.

"Don't be jealous."

Tommy laughs, but Mike doesn't seem to notice. He's too busy surveying the crowd. "What's with all these women?"

"She does a lotta lesbo stuff," Robby says.

Mike seems intrigued. "Really?"

"Oh, yeah," Robby says. "Total switch-hitter. And not just the ol' 'take it and fake it', either. She apparently *loves* getting her carpet cleaned."

Mike looks at Nikki and smiles. I could swear I see him

lick his lips in anticipation - of exactly what I'm not sure.

"That's relatively new," Charlie says in his scholarly way, "the whole lesbian thing - one Butch, one Femme, anyway. Used to be it was a 'warm up' for the man. But not anymore. Not since feminism, I guess."

Robby shakes his head. "Couldn't leave well enough alone, could they?"

"Actually, there's *always* been a lot of Sapphic imagery in artwork," I say. "If you look back at -"

Everyone stops and stares at me. Only then do I realize what I said. "Seriously," I add.

Robby looks at me like I'm an alien. "'Sapphic'? What the hell is that?"

Tommy steps forward. "Sappho ... the poet. Lived on Lesbos. Wrote love poems to Aphrodite ... right?" He looks at me. I nod. I remember all this from English class.

Robby doesn't believe it. "You two are so full of shit. Lesbos? Really ..."

Tommy shrugs, smiles, and shares a look of solidarity with me. It's a nice moment and makes me feel not so self-conscious about what I said. But I doubt I'll say anything else like that - not in this environment.

Around the time Nikki finishes signing for the last customer, Mike prepares to leave.

"All right, Bro," he says to me, "you ready to rock and roll, help me get set up?"

I look at the clock. "I'm not done yet."

"It's okay, Bri," Tommy says. I think it's the first time he's ever used my name, especially in such a familiar way. "I'll cover for you."

"You sure?" I say. Tommy nods. "Thanks."

I gather my things while Mike goes over to say goodbye to Nikki. "It was very nice to meet you," he says. "I'll see you later." She forces a smile.

I follow Mike out.

At the door, I turn to see Tommy lead Nikki to the back room. Again I wonder if there's something strange going on ... and if maybe that's the reason Tommy said it was okay for me to end work early. But I leave before I get a chance to find out.

I'm probably just making it all up in my head, anyway.

The birthday celebration Mike throws for himself turns out to be one hell of a party. Guys are drinking, carousing, and letting loose like animals released from a cage.

There are no girls there; only women - the strippers Mr. Welch hired. Plus Nikki. They're all dancing with the guests, prompting them to give money for lap dances or whatever, but mostly they focus on Mike. And he's only too happy to give them all the money he has to keep their attention. He's in heaven ... or his version of it, anyway. I suppose it's a lot of guys'.

All I can think about is how it wasn't too long ago that Mike was chewing gum and blowing bubbles on a Little League pitcher's mound, barely even aware of girls. Now he's getting full on, grinding lap dances from half-naked women and no doubt hoping for more than that - as always.

Of course, I could, too ... if I wanted. I'm not really interested, though. I know it sounds hard to believe, but it just doesn't appeal to me, the whole "getting teased by women you're not gonna have sex with" thing. Even if they wanted to have sex, that's the last thing I'd do, as long as I have Jennifer.

Still, they try to tempt me, if only for the money. So I tell them I don't have any. That seems to work. To the one it doesn't work on, I say, "I have a girlfriend."

"That's sweet," she says and continues to rub against me.

I must admit, it does turn me on. And I'm a little tempted to take out some money for a dance. But still, I know it's not going anywhere, at least not without me being forced to spend more money than I'd be willing to - or can at this point. And I'm certainly not going to do that when I can be with someone I care about for free.

So I excuse myself and walk away. She doesn't seem to care and simply moves on to another potential customer as I step over to the corner of the room, out of the way.

I watch the goings-on for a bit and it really starts to creep me out - maybe even worse than some of the things I've seen at Adult World. At least there, it's kind of all around, par for the course. In your average suburban living room, it's just weird.

I'm not sure what's worse: the guys waiting turns to pay women to rub up against them for five minutes or the women themselves, who are, sorry to say, not all that pretty. I mean, Nikki's not bad and maybe the others, the local ones, would be under different circumstances. But here? Not so much.

As the scene gets more bizarre, I consider how I would paint it. At first I think of van Gogh and his darker mood interiors and portraits, but when I zero in on the specific forms moving this way and that at all angles, I quickly realize that Picasso's the way to go - specifically, in his later years, when he was mixing cubist and surreal elements. I suppose the scene could also be captured in the style of his Blue Period, when it really comes down to it. It is kind of sad.

I wonder why it seems so many women have little respect for themselves. But that might just be a result of the places I've been spending time lately. I've seen a lot of men with little respect for themselves, too. Even less respect for women. I guess it's kind of a vicious cycle.

I decide I've seen enough and go to get a drink. As I walk to the kitchen, I see that Rick Schmidt has arrived. We nod a cold hello to each other.

I'm actually glad to see him. At least I know he's not with Jennifer, although I have no real reason to suspect he would be. But there's no accounting for insecurity and fear, I guess.

It's also nice to know that I now have something against Rick if I should ever need it. But then again, he has something on me, too. So I think maybe it'd be a good idea to leave early and see Jennifer - especially since I'm still a little turned on from the dancer, despite how I want to feel about it. I'm not completely immune to temptation ... and again, once the launch-sequence has begun, it really takes on a life of its own.

I find a quiet room and use the new phone Mr. Welch gave me to call her. Thankfully, she answers. We chat a little before I tell her where I am - leaving out the stripper part, of course - and that I want to come and see her.

"Not necessarily in that order," I say, then laugh in case she thinks I'm being too crude.

I think she's okay with the innuendo, though, because I can hear her smiling as she tells me to come over. I say I will as soon as I can. I don't want to just cut out; it is my best friend's birthday party, after all.

Thankfully, as I return to the living room, I see Mike being led out to another room by Nikki - so it won't matter if I split. Mike won't even know I'm gone - at least not for a while. And by then I doubt he'll even care.

After I leave Mike's birthday party, I pick up Jennifer and we go back to my house, since my mom's out on a date with Gary.

We hang out for a little in the living room, like we usually do, and I listen as she tells me about her day and how much fun she had babysitting her two-year-old niece. I'm only too happy to let her talk, so I can avoid mentioning what was really going on at Mike's party.

In the middle of her story about how she was using crayons to color in pictures with her niece and thought of me, she jerks to attention, like she's just realized something - which she has.

"Oh, I wanna see the drawings," she says, excited. "The ones from the other day, when you were on the bleachers."

I freeze. I'm not sure I want to show them to her yet.

She can no doubt read the hesitation on my face. "C'mon. You promised."

"I know, but ... they're not finished." Actually, they're pretty close, but I figure if I have to show them to her, I better set the bar low. I think they're pretty good, but you never know what others are going to think.

"It's okay," she says. "I just wanna see."

"Really?"

"Of course. I wanna see everything you've done. You never let me."

She looks so sweet and eager, it's hard to say no. I resist a little more, but am totally won over when she lays her best pleading puppy-dog eyes on me.

Before I can even say, "Okay," she's jumping up and down giddily.

It's so cute I just wanna give her a big hug.

I shake my head, smile, take a deep breath, and head upstairs to my room to get the pastels.

Jennifer bounds up from the couch and follows me.

I stop on the stairs. "What are you doing?"

"Coming with you."

It's not like it's the first time she's ever seen my room, but usually I hide all my unfinished artwork, or the stuff that I don't want her to see, before she comes over.

Tonight, her eager, happy face relaxes me somehow and I'm not afraid that she'll make fun of anything she sees.

I don't know why I ever thought she would in the first place. I guess because it's a scary thing revealing a part of yourself, which is what the best art does - or should do. I hope mine does, too … if only a little.

It isn't until she walks into my room that I realize there's something else I *definitely* don't want her to see: my Adult World staff shirts, one of which is sitting on my bureau. I snatch it, toss it out of site in my clothes hamper, and do a quick sweep of the room to make sure there's nothing else incriminating for her to see.

It looks fine, but I sit her down on the bed where her field of vision is limited, just in case. I then take out the pastel sketches I made from the cheerleader sketches, put them in order of best to worst, discard the last one, which I don't like so much, and hand them to her.

Her eyes widen as she looks, then she opens her mouth and inhales loudly.

"Oh, my God."

She clearly likes what I've done. *Whew!*

"These are amazing," she says as I join her on the bed. "Wow."

She gets to the last one, which is an image of her, although with the haze of pastel, it's hard to tell exactly. Still, I think she knows.

She looks up at me, her mouth open in awe. "You're amazing."

I blush at the compliment and want to kiss her. In fact, as usual, I want to do even more than that and tell myself I earned it with that last pastel.

But she doesn't seem in the mood. I think she's more interested in seeing my artwork than getting physical.

"What else do you have?" she asks as she stands, looks around the room, and zeroes in on a group of canvases leaning upright against the wall next to my bed.

I hid them in the closet every other time she came over because they're older works and not very original. I painted them a while ago, when I was experimenting with a variety of styles, depending on which one I was trying to learn at the time.

It's interesting what you can learn by putting on different artist's hats. I guess I'm still doing it, with my Degas-inspired sketches. But, if you're gonna learn, you might as well learn - or steal - from the best.

Jennifer flips through my artist sampler pack and pulls out one particularly vivid work that stands taller than the rest. It's a vertical image of a sunset over a razor-thin horizon at the bottom, with a sky that gradually darkens to almost black as it reaches the top of the canvas. I painted it in a Post-Impressionist style, with thick, short strokes to copy van Gogh's technique.

Not bad, I think as I look at it again.

"I like this," she says.

"Yeah?"

She nods. "Kinda like van Gogh, right?"

"Right. That's what I was going for, anyway."

"You did a good job," she says with a smile, then stares at the painting a little longer and puts it back. "I did a report on him in the seventh grade. So sad."

"Why do you say that?"

"He was really lonely."

"So they say ... but look at all the masterpieces he created. Maybe that's what made him who he is ... or was."

She remains silent a few moments as she looks at some of my other works, then says, "I don't think it's worth the trade off."

I have no response for her.

"Don't you think?" she asks and looks up from the paintings.

"I don't know. I mean, I think it would be nice to have a gift like that, something you're remembered for."

"Why do you have to be remembered? Isn't it enough just to have it ... y'know, while you're alive?"

"I guess. But it would be nice if people knew who you were ... what you were doing ... what you thought ... and saw - or the way you saw it - after you're gone."

"You could always have children," she says. "Then you'd be remembered. *They'd* remember you."

"Maybe ... but there's no guarantee of that. Look at my dad; I barely remember him. And that might just be from the pictures my mom has of him."

For some reason I get a little choked up. It catches me by surprise and I try to hide it, but I think she notices because she smiles sympathetically and says, "Sure you do. You just mentioned him."

"I know, but -"

Before I can continue, she leans in and kisses me so deeply, so passionately, that it removes all the sadness from me in an instant. Her intensity surprises me. It's stronger than it's ever been before. I'm not sure why, but have to figure it has something to do with me showing some emotion, some vulnerability, which I did. And under different circumstances I'd be completely self-conscious about it. But here, with her, I feel safe. It's nice. I think it makes me even more turned on, too, just like it appears to have done for her.

We get really physical and grasp at each other like starving kids in a candy store. And I want to sample everything I can. Maybe it's the intimacy ... or maybe it was all the talk about Nikki earlier ... or it might just be my desire to return the favor for what Jennifer's done to me many times already, but this time, after I explore her with my fingers and before she can go down on me, I slide down and try to pull her pants all the way off.

"What are you doing?" she asks.

"I'm just gonna ..." I tilt my head toward below her waist to let her know my intention.

She wiggles away and pushes on my head. "No, no. Don't."

"Whatsamatter?"

"I, I ... just, don't ..."

"Why not?" I don't understand why she won't let me do to her what she's done to me.

"Stop pushing me," she says.

"I'm not pushing. I just want to ... make you ... feel good."

"I know. I'm sorry. I'm just, I'm not ready for that."

I must be going too fast. Still, it's not like I could get her pregnant or take her virginity with this or anything.

Maybe she feels like it'll cheapen the intimacy of a few minutes ago, though.

Whatever her reason, I don't want to push her into anything she doesn't want. So I stop and ease back into physical contact. I put my hand on her again and move it up and down.

"Is this okay?"

She nods. She seems to enjoy what I'm doing and the more excited she gets, the faster and firmer I move my hand. She even moves her hips to position my fingers where it feels best and loses herself in the pleasure. At least I think she does. I'm pretty sure she even has an orgasm eventually, although I can't tell for sure. It's not like a guy's, where there's clear evidence.

So after things calm down I ask her. "Did you … y'know?"

She nods, but I'm still not sure and don't have much time to think about it, because in a matter of moments she goes down on me again. And it's incredible. It feels better this time than ever before.

Still, a few minutes after I've finished, when some clarity returns to my head, I wonder about what she felt - and whether she told me the truth about it.

The next day at work, I still feel good about getting closer to Jennifer, but can't shake the uncertainty over just what she felt physically. So I ask Tommy about it.

I don't get too specific, though, and don't mention Jennifer by name or anything. Just kind of in a general sense. Hypothetically. But I'm sure he figures I'm talking about her.

"That's a hard thing to tell," he says. "Were you working the clit?"

I try not to look like I'm answering one way or the other and wait for him to continue.

"'Cause if you wanna get her off, man, ya gotta work the clit," he says. "You know where that is, right?"

I nod, but it's clear I'm not sure. I don't think I'll ever be.

I mean, I kind of know what he's talking about, but only in the theoretical sense, from the sex books I've read in school, or during my own research at the bookstore and on the Internet. I've been reading as much as I can since I started getting physical with Jennifer.

"Well, just find the little man in the boat," Tommy says, "and you'll be fine."

I'm still not sure what he's talking about. *Man? Boat?*

I turn to see Robby come in and try to look busy, so Tommy will let the subject drop. The last thing I want is for Robby to get involved.

But Tommy keeps going with it. "Use your tongue, your finger ... Hell, your big toe. Whatever you got. Find it and work it."

Too late; Robby's heard him. "What are you talking about?"

"Nothing," I say.

"How women fake it sometimes," Tommy says.

"Oh," Robby says. "Pfft. Why they think they have to is beyond me. I mean, who really cares? As long as you're getting yours. Right?"

Tommy looks at me and shrugs, as if telling me silently not to listen to Robby. It's a look I've seen many times since I started working with the two of them. Thankfully, the subject is dropped and we all get back to work.

Then Robby adds, "Hey, y'know the word 'orgasm' comes from the French. It means 'little death'."

Tommy gives me that same look again, shakes his head at Robby, and says, "Oh, shut up."

"It's true. I read it in a magazine. Or maybe it was in a movie ... But look it up."

"Yeah. And the word 'gullible' isn't in the dictionary." Tommy smirks.

"What do you mean?"

Tommy dismisses him with a shake of his head and turns back to me. "The clit, Brian. Trust me. The clit."

I nod and think about it. Then I decide, *What the hell; we're talking. I might as well ask about other stuff along this same line.*

"What about the G-spot?" I've read about it in a few books.

"Don't worry about that," Tommy says. "It's a myth - like The Loch Ness Monster or The Yeti."

"Or that women want sex as much as we do," Robby adds.

"Really? From what I've read -"

"'Read'? Now you sound like Robby. Where'd you read it? *Penthouse Forum*?"

"No. This was a book, a sex book. It's supposed to be a sensitive area behind the front wall of the vagina that can stimulate an orgasm. It apparently triggers the release of fluid from the urethra, too."

Robby's face curls. "What are you talkin' about? Piss?"

"No. It's, um, vaginal fluid. Like semen."

"So, what, women have sperm?"

Tommy again shakes his head. "No, dummy. Semen only *carries* the sperm. He's talking about something similar to ejaculation."

I nod.

"And how do you make that happen?" Robby asks.

"It said you can use your finger," I say.

While we're talking, I notice Mr. Welch enter the store and go into the back. We all pause a moment to, at the very least, look like we're working, until he's gone.

Tommy stands as if to follow, but stops when Robby says, "Hey, you hear about the woman who went into the drugstore and asked where the batteries were? The druggist nods and says, 'come this way'." Robby holds out his index finger and curls it. "And the woman says, 'If I could come that way, I wouldn't need the batteries ...'"

I laugh. It's not a bad joke - and one I may not have fully understood until I started working at Adult World.

Tommy shakes his head. It's obvious he's heard it before. He looks at me and says, "I'm tellin' ya: The clit. It's a helluva lot easier to find." Tommy then looks at Robby and says, "'Little death.' Pfft. Moron ..." before he goes into the back where Mr. Welch is.

A few minutes later, Mike enters Adult World puffed up and strutting like a rooster. "Bro, what happened to you last night?" he says when he sees me.

I don't want to tell him I saw Jennifer, but it's probably clear from my indifferent shrug.

"What the fuck? You ditch me on my birthday?"

I do feel bad about it, so I invoke the Nookie Clause.

"Yeah, I figured," he says with an accepting nod. "Well, you missed an awesome time. You at least get some of that nookie you're clausing me on?"

I shrug again. I don't want to tell him. I'm beginning to maybe see why Tommy shrugs so much. Sometimes it's just easier.

"Man, she has you wrapped around her little finger, doesn't she?" Mike says.

"From what I hear, it's the other way around ..." Robby mutters with a laugh.

Just then, Tommy comes out with his jacket on, ready to leave, and sees Mike. "Well, if it ain't Superfly himself. How'd your little play-date with Nikki go last night?"

Mike's proud grin amps up to "shit-eating" level and I find out why he looks so proud. "Let's put it this way," he says. "What has two thumbs and loves to eat pussy?" Mike points both thumbs at himself. "This guy."

An even bigger grin than Mike's rises on Tommy's face. "You went down on her?" He says it in a surprisingly cheerful way - cheerful for Tommy, that is.

Mike flicks his tongue. "The only way to fly."

Tommy laughs and Robby's face curls.

"Made her crazy, too," Mike says, then stops when he sees that Tommy and Robby are looking at him strangely. "What?"

"Oh, Spanky, Spanky, Spanky," Tommy says like a teacher speaking to an ignorant student. "She lets me do her here, then you go and ... that's like ... licking *me*."

"Shut up," Mike says. "Liar."

Tommy looks at Robby to confirm his story for Mike. Robby nods and shakes his head at Mike with mock apology.

After staring at them both for a few blank seconds, Mike dismisses them with a wave of his hand. "Eh, even if you did, I'm sure you wore a rubber."

"Yeah," Tommy says, "but that doesn't cover *everything*."

Robby jumps and exaggerates a chill going through his body. "Ew! So his balls were slappin' right about where your lower lip was!" He cracks up.

Mike seems to consider the notion. His face wrenches in disgust, but he fights it, I guess to not be embarrassed any further.

Through his laughter, Robby says, "Hah! You were a carpet cleaner after he was a carpet *bagger!* Get it?"

Tommy laughs louder than I've ever heard him do anything.

I fight the urge to, myself. I don't want to throw salt on my best friend's wound.

"I'm sure she at least washed up, Mike," I say. "I mean, before you -"

"Oh, sure," Tommy says seriously. "'Cause her first obligation is to some horny high-schooler."

He and Robby launch into raucous laughter again.

Mike seems to search for some sort of response, something to prove that they're lying, or at least make them think it doesn't matter to him, but it's clear he can't. All he can muster through the embarrassment is, "Fuck you guys." He then turns and leaves in a huff.

I feel bad for him. His good time - depraved as it was, if it's even true - is now ruined, regardless of whether Tommy and Robby are telling the truth, themselves. And they very well may not be. They could be just saying all that stuff to fuck with Mike.

"Aw, that wasn't nice," I say to them.

Tommy smirks. "Ah, I know he's your friend and all, but the little fucker deserves it ... thinkin' he owns the place ..."

I can kind of see Tommy's point. If I were him I'd probably have the same attitude about Mike. If you don't know him like I know him, he might wear on you a little.

Still, he didn't need that. He was a boy playing in a game of men. And he lost.

It certainly makes me feel better about my own reluctance to jump into that game. That's for sure.

That night I sneak into my house and go right to the kitchen to wash my hands - as I always do after working in Adult World - before I eat some dinner. My mom's sitting at the table, reading her *Woman's World* magazine - or pretending to, anyway.

We say hello.

She asks me how my day was.

I say it was fine.

Then, once I have a plateful of food out of the microwave and sit to eat, she says, "So ... I stopped by Truman's today." She then does that thing where she waits and watches to see if I react.

Moms all probably do the same thing. And they can see any reaction you might have, no matter how minute, to extract the truth from you.

Still, I believe I'm pretty good with my simple response of a casual nod as I continue to focus on my meal.

"They said you don't work there anymore. Haven't for weeks."

I nod again, as if to say, *"Yeah. Of course. You know that already. No big deal."*

She doesn't know, of course, but can no doubt tell that something's up.

"What happened? Did you get fired?"

"No."

She looks at me, waiting for more.

"I, I sorta got a, another job," I say. "A better-paying

job."

"Why didn't you tell me?"

"Well, I, uh, wasn't sure you'd be happy knowing what I'm doing, per se." There I am with the *per se* again.

What is that? Why do I say that when I'm trying to keep from telling the truth?

"Oh. What are you doing?"

I take as much time as possible before I tell her, then spit it out nonchalantly. "Working for Mr. Welch."

She doesn't seem to understand. "Really? And what're you - ?" Then her shoulders drop and her face goes blank. "No. Not *there.*"

I shrug apologetically, but quickly realize I don't want to look sorry. If I do, then it looks like I've done something bad. And I haven't, really.

Still, it's hard to counter her look of disappointment. But I try.

"I make a lot more there than I did at Truman's," I say. "How else am I supposed to pay for school?"

Her disappointment for me vanishes in an instant and is replaced by something that almost looks like disappointment in *herself.* She remains speechless. How can she possibly argue with me, since I have to pay for college myself?

"It's not so bad," I say to ease her fears that I may be corrupted by the experience or something. "I actually -"

"Okay, okay," she says. "You're old enough. It's your choice. I just, I don't want to hear about it."

I could have sworn she was going to cover her ears and make a "na-na-na-na-na" sound with her mouth, like a child.

I feel bad that I used her financial shortcoming against her, but say nothing more about it and go back to my dinner.

After she watches me take a few bites, she says, "It's all legal, right?"

"Yeah. It's a legitimate business."

"Okay. I hope you're right."

I don't know why she would say that. I've never seen anything illegal go on. It's a business, like any other.

Yeah, Mr. Welch knows strippers and sometimes hires them to perform for people at parties, but that's legal, isn't it? I'm pretty sure it is.

Yeah. It's gotta be.

It's not like they have sex with guys - at least I don't think so.

Nah. Mr. Welch wouldn't do that. He wouldn't break the law ... and risk losing his business - especially with the way he used to get on Mike, his own son, for merely being in Adult World when he was underage.

Okay, so maybe Nikki did something with Mike and maybe she did something with Tommy and Robby.

Maybe.

I don't know that for sure. For all I know they're all full of shit and none of it happened. It's quite possible. Probable, even. Guys lie about that stuff all the time, don't they?

And if someone skirts the outer limits of the law, as long as I'm not, what do I care?

Either way, I'm just happy I don't have to hide my staff shirt or lie to my mom about going to Truman's anymore. I have enough to worry about at the moment - namely, my future.

FIFTH

On Monday morning I make a point to show up early at the baseball field to be certain I see Mike and find out how he's doing after the embarrassment of his episode with Nikki. He shows up, but after a quick nod hello he's unusually silent as he sits and smokes his cigarette.

"You all right?" I ask.

He calmly flicks ash to the ground. "Whaddya mean? Why wouldn't I be?"

"Eh, y'know, the whole Nikki thing."

He smirks and shakes his head. "Yeah. Fine."

I nod and let the subject die in the morning silence.

After a few minutes, he says, "Y'know, you coulda told me."

"Sorry. But I didn't even know. I mean, I *thought* ... maybe ... but I figured you didn't care. It's not like she's your girlfriend or something."

This doesn't seem to comfort Mike. I can tell he feels like I betrayed him somehow. And although I know it's in no way my fault, I still feel bad about it.

"Ah, they were probably just fucking with you,

anyway."

Mike nods. "Yeah … you're probably right."

It may indeed be true. And if it isn't, I hope he believes it is, anyway. To be honest, I kind of want to believe that, myself - because if Tommy did what he said he did … and Mike did what he said *he* did … *Ick.*

Mike shakes his head, takes another draw of his cigarette, drops it to the ground, and grinds it to shreds with his foot. "Fuckin' losers. I'm gonna own them some day. I'll show 'em. Heh. Just wait 'til Holly comes."

"Who's that?" I ask.

Holly is Holly Silva, yet another adult film actress - although, according to Robby, she's on a whole other level than the rest. She's gone mainstream and is like an A-list movie star in the world of adult films. She's also one of the few "actresses" who gets a percentage of the profits on her movies and, between products and appearances, easily makes over a million dollars a year. A *million* dollars … for porn! Only in America …

But as big as she is, I've still never heard of her - maybe because I don't pay attention to that stuff. I suppose I'll get to know who she is on May Seventh, though. That's when she's coming to Adult World.

I think Robby already has a boner just thinking about it. The day he hangs up the poster announcing the event, I even see him kiss her image.

"Holly Silva, you sweet piece of cake, you," he says, then turns to me, unashamed of his fawning over a photograph. "Fuck, I can't wait for her."

"What's she selling?" I ask him.

"A rubber mold of her snatch."

I love Robby's directness. Crude, but effective. I laugh at the thought of people buying such a thing.

"Laugh all you want," he says, "but it'll sell like hotcakes. She's a fucking star. Check it out."

Robby puts on a video of her and I gotta admit, she definitely looks sexy - even with the bad lighting of the movie. There aren't the usual pock, stretch, or acne marks on her skin like there are on most actresses in the movies I've seen in Adult World. I wonder if they do digital correction on them - and whether the type of person who usually buys these things even cares.

I know I do. The nicer they look, the more artistic the images, the more I like it. It must be the visual artist in me.

"Whaddya think?" Robby asks.

She may be hot, but in all her photos and movies she still has that overly made-up, slutty look I don't like. That and ... she's a porn actress.

"She's all right ... I guess."

"You tellin' me you wouldn't do that?" he asks with a smirk.

I shrug.

"Ah, you're fulla shit," he says. "She put that twat in your face, you'd cream all over yourself."

I could be wrong, but I honestly don't think I would.

"Fuck, even the boss would do that - and he doesn't like to mix business and pleasure. Well, except for that black girl, whatever her name is."

"Angela?"

"Yeah. That's it."

"She's a stripper?" I ask. I didn't get the feeling she was when I met her.

"No. She's one of his tenants," Robby says, then

laughs. "Funny how she comes around whenever the rent's due. I hear she lets him take pictures of her. He digs that …"

"Get outta here. Mr. Welch? Really?"

"Oh, yeah. I've seen 'em, too - not of her, but others. He's got a whole collection. Some kind of power thing, I guess - y'know, like those native tribes that think you steal someone's soul when you take their picture or something."

I wouldn't have thought that about Mr. Welch. I'm still not sure I believe it. Who knows what kinds of stories Robby makes up?

I don't get much of a chance to think about it because as I talk to Robby, the front door opens and in strolls Mr. Kinney. That's right; Jennifer's dad is in the store!

I don't know if he's there as a customer or if he found out I work there or something, but I don't wait around to find out. I immediately drop behind the counter.

Robby must think I tripped or something, because he grabs my arm to help me up. I tug against it and shake my head.

"Whatsamatter? What are you - ?"

"Shh. I'm not here," I whisper, then watch the security video monitors to see what Mr. Kinney does. To my surprise, he goes through the store and picks up a few items like any other customer.

After about five or ten minutes - although it seems like a hell of a lot longer than that - he comes up to the register to buy the items. By then I'm well-hidden in the back room, peeking through the slightly open door and waiting for him to finish getting rung up.

When he's gone, I come out again.

Robby looks at me, puzzled. "You know him or something?"

"That's my girlfriend's dad."

Robby laughs. "Get out!"

"Seriously."

"I've seen him in here a buncha times."

"He's, like, the Deacon of his church."

"Heh," Robby says and goes back to work. "That figures ..."

"What'd he buy?"

"I don't know. The usual: coupla videos, magazines - mostly bondage stuff."

"No way!" I'm having a tough time wrapping my brain around this.

"Yeah. Kinky ol' fucker, I guess."

"But he's married."

"So? Maybe she doesn't do it for him. Or maybe she likes it frrrrrreaky ..." Robby makes a whipping motion with his arm. "Wah-tsh!"

"I don't even wanna *think* about that," I say as a creepy shiver runs outward from my core.

"Hey, we all have a little of that in us. Just gotta let it out."

I think maybe Robby's right. If someone like Mr. Kinney can be into stuff like that, who knows who else is?

Who knows anything about anybody, really?

As freaked out as I am about seeing Mr. Kinney, I gotta say there's a thrill in knowing he comes into Adult World and buys a lot of kinky stuff - especially after all that morality talk and the hedonism spiel at Easter dinner. Kinda takes him down a peg - or raises me up one. I'm not sure which is which, or if either is necessarily a good thing.

The one thing I know is I'm not gonna feel so damn self-conscious the next time I see him. People like that, who claim to be on higher moral ground than the rest of us, have a way of doing that to a person - even when there's no real justification for it.

And now that I know what I know, I have nothing to be ashamed of anymore.

A week or so later, I'm at Jennifer's house, her parents are out, and we're getting physical again - only this time I'm even more aggressive than normal. Well, aggressive sounds kind of negative. It's more like "amorous." That's better, right? *Amor. Love.*

It is love, too … I think. I've never felt about anybody the way I feel about Jennifer. Each day it seems to get stronger.

And my feelings have definitely made me want to be more physical with her, to do more than we have so far. I want the home run. I'm not sure she feels the same way, though … at least she doesn't this night.

"My parents are going to be home soon," she says as she pushes me away with a laugh.

"So? They won't care."

"Yeah, right. My dad would freak."

I laugh. I want to say, "Your dad *is* a freak," and I think maybe I do, under my breath. I'm not sure.

"What?" Jennifer asks.

"I didn't say anything."

I kiss her again and stroke her breast to distract her from the subject. It seems to work. She goes along with me, despite the possibility of her parents coming home - or maybe because of it - and soon my hand is on her, my fingers in her.

I love feeling her writhe with excitement beneath me. Still, like always, I want to do something more to turn up the heat and make it better for her. This time I just happen to be prepared with something new.

I don't know what made me think this would work - maybe the job is warping my brain - but tonight I've brought a vibrator from the store with me. Not a big one. A very small one, in fact. It's called a Butterfly and is about the size of a really thin egg, but with wings on either side. It's powered by a single AA battery, so it's not like it's industrial strength or anything.

I figure it'll at least help with the finger stimulation, especially since she still won't let me go down on her - to say nothing of actually having sex.

I suppose I should say "intercourse"; we've been having "sex" for a while now. And since we have to stick to ways of giving each other pleasure short of intercourse, I guess I feel the need to get creative.

"Here," I say and take out the Butterfly. "I brought something ..." She probably can't see it in the dim light, but when I get it near her and turn it on, she can clearly hear it.

"What are you ... ?" She pushes my hand away. "What is that?!"

"Just a little something to help you ... y'know ..." I say.

She pushes me away again. "Get that away from me!"

I turn it off as she turns on the lights and stares at me in shock.

I don't know what to say. I didn't think it was as big a deal as she seems to think. From what I've seen, they're very common. A lot of women, girls too, use them - on themselves.

Still, I don't like the look she gives me - like I've done something wrong in trying to make her feel good. "Well, what am I supposed to do?" I say.

"I don't know. Not *that*!"

"Don't you want to ... ?" I let the sentence trail off. She knows what I'm talking about - her climaxing. I'm still not sure she has.

Most people my age probably don't care about that, but I do. I don't know why. Maybe it's a power thing. Maybe I just want her to feel as vulnerable as I do when I have one.

"Yes. You know I do," she answers. I think she means have sex, though - not just orgasm. And that's fine, too. I mean, I'd rather do *that* first. "I don't want to do it *here*, though," she says.

"Then when?" I say. I don't mean to; I know it sounds like I'm pressuring her. I think I'm just embarrassed at having brought the Butterfly. I think guys sometimes sound angrier than we are when we feel awkward. It's kind of our only defense.

But I don't want her to think I'm angry. "I'm sorry," I say. "I just, I, I want to be with you." And it's the truth. It's not about the sex as much as it is about having sex *with her*. I want her to be my first.

Either she doesn't mind or I said the right thing, because she smiles at me and says, "The prom's coming up, y'know."

"Yeah?"

She nods and says, "I'll be able to stay out," followed by a seductive smile and eyebrow arch.

A wave of thrilling anticipation flows through me and I'm compelled to get closer to her. In no time we get physical again. It seems more intense now and at one point she even seems to indicate that she wants me to go down on her.

I don't want to push my luck by assuming that's what she means, especially with the after-prom plan we just made at stake. But when she gently pushes down on my shoulders while sliding her body up on the bed, I know I'm reading her loud and clear.

Maybe she feels bad about stopping my attempt to make her feel good with the Butterfly and wants to make it up to me now.

If so, who am I to deny her that?

So I work my way slowly down to put my mouth on her and I gotta say, when I finally do, it's so much better than I ever thought it would be. She tastes both sweet and sour on my tongue and feels warm and soft against my lips.

It's amazing.

Of course, I might just feel this way because I'm so happy about joining Jennifer on third base. She got there first way back on Easter Sunday, after dinner at her parents' house, and has been standing there on her own since then.

At least that's what I've decided: the person who *does* it is the one who gets the base.

But none of that matters anymore, because we're both safe on third now.

I'm not sure exactly what I'm supposed to do, but have seen enough of this stuff in videos to get a general idea.

Like Tommy said, I focus on the clitoris - that is, if it's where I think it is.

His words echo in my head: "Find the little man in the boat."

If he meant what I think he meant, and if I'm to believe the diagrams I've seen, the "little man" is at the top. So I keep my tongue mostly there.

I've also seen guys in videos use their fingers at the same time as their mouths, so I do that, too. I can tell she likes it, because she not only seems to lose more control than she has in the past, but also lets me linger there for longer than I would have expected.

Around the time my jaw begins to ache, I think she's just about to finish. But before she does, I feel her hands on my shoulders to pull me back up to her. I'm not sure why and don't respond right away.

She pulls again, though, and I'm forced to stop what I'm doing, albeit reluctantly. I move back up so we're face to face again, but make sure I leave my hand behind.

She doesn't seem to mind, so I continue to move my fingers in and out for a few minutes while I kiss her wherever I can on her upper torso. She eventually loses complete control and has an orgasm.

At least I think she does. I've never heard her make that much noise before. Plus, it feels different to me, tighter on my fingers. Wetter, too. That's gotta mean something.

"Wow. That felt *soooo* good," she purrs and stretches as if just waking from a nap.

I want to ask her if she really finished, but figure it's probably a subject best left alone.

"Do you want me to do something for you?" she asks, although I can tell she's not really in the mood at this point. As turned on as I am, I decide to let her relax and enjoy the feeling like she's done for me so many times before.

"That's okay," I say. "I'm fine."

And I am. Better than fine, in fact. I'm great.

Better than great, even. Perfect.

Not only have I joined Jennifer on third base, but now it looks like she's running toward home and beckoning for me to follow. If all goes well, after the prom we'll get there together.

I feel like I'm walking on air when I give Jennifer a kiss goodnight at her front door. I float toward my car, grinning like a canary that just ate a cat - a lion, even - as Mr. and Mrs. Kinney pull into the driveway and get out of their car.

"Hi, Mr. Kinney," I say, then nod my head to his wife like a cowboy tipping his hat. "Mrs. Kinney."

I was right before; all my self-consciousness and insecurity around Mr. Kinney has evaporated. It feels fantastic.

I can sense his curiosity at my new attitude as I walk to my car.

"Brian," he says.

I stop and turn around. "Yes?"

"A word?"

I walk right up to him as Mrs. Kinney passes Jennifer on her way into the house. Jennifer looks at me with some concern, but I wink at her to let her know it's okay.

She smiles, nods, and follows her mom inside.

"What's up, Mr. K?"

He squints, as if trying to read my mind. "You remember what we talked about?"

"Absolutely," I say, then get a perverse notion in my head. "You might say it *dominates* my thoughts." I know it's like playing with fire, but I can't help it.

Try as he will, Mr. Kinney still can't read my mind. He seems thrown by my confidence.

"So we still understand each other."

"Yessir," I say. "Clearly. Crystal clearly." I look him in the eye and wait for more. He looks puzzled as to why he's lost his ability to intimidate me.

I fight my urge to smile and say a polite, "Well, goodnight," then turn and walk away. Only then does the smile I've been holding in announce itself on my face. He's gotta be able to see it, even from behind.

I'm smiling not only because I feel powerful against Mr. Kinney now and am solidly on third base, but also because I know that in a few short weeks, when the prom comes - and if all goes well - I will be *with* Jennifer for the first time.

The only exciting - and I use that term lightly, considering how I feel about it - thing to happen between now and the prom is Holly Silva's visit to the store. I assume it's going to be no different than the other porn actress visits.

This time, though, I've told myself I'm going to pay close attention to what Tommy and Robby do with Holly - if they do anything. I want to know for sure if they've been making up all this shit about having sex with the actresses in the back room - which is what I suspect.

I once even looked for stains on the couch back there, but the place is so disorganized and the couch so old to begin with, it was already a mess.

Yeah, I know it's disgusting, but we're talking about biological processes here and I suppose part of being an adult is learning to be comfortable with that sort of thing. I mean, one day, I'll probably do much worse - like change diapers or something like that.

My mom told me about how she once had to suck the snot out of my nose with a straw when I was a baby - because I was too young to be able to blow it out. Can you imagine?

But if it was your own baby, your own flesh and blood, or someone you love, all that probably wouldn't matter.

Hell, if you told me a few years ago about all the things I'd eventually do - and want to do - with Jennifer, I wouldn't have believed you. No way, no how.

But here I am.

And there I intend to go.

SIXTH

The turnout for Holly Silva at Adult World is surprising. The store is packed way more than I've ever seen it. Outside, there's even a line of customers who can't come in because too many people inside would violate the building's fire code. It's crazy.

"See?" Robby says. "I told you. A star."

I'm still not buying the notion that she's anything special, but am curious to see her in the flesh when she arrives. All these people must be there for a reason.

Everyone has to work hard with so many customers and I notice that Charlie's not there to help this time. He's always at the store when there's a "celebrity" visit. And most weekends when nobody's coming he at least pops in and hangs out for an hour or two.

"Hey. Where's Charlie?" I ask.

"I don't know," Tommy says. "Hasn't been around in a while, has he?"

"You think he's okay? We'd know if something bad happened to him, right?"

Tommy shrugs. "I doubt it. I don't think he's got any

family. If he did, I doubt they'd know about him coming in here."

"That's true," I say and continue to wonder if he's okay.

He's kind of a strange guy, Charlie. I think the people at Adult World are his only friends. And I can't even call them - us - that. He mostly just hung out and talked pornography. He seemed kind of lonely and I feel bad for him. I know a little about how hard loneliness can be and fear maybe he did something drastic. Like, maybe he's hanging by a rope in his apartment - and has been for weeks. But nobody knows, because nobody visits or calls.

Before I can suggest that maybe someone at least call him to check if he's okay, a customer approaches the register and asks, "Is one of you Brian?"

I look at him curiously, then nod.

"A girl outside's asking for you," he says.

I can't imagine who it might be. My first thought is that it's my mom, but she's not exactly a girl.

"How old is she?" I ask.

"Old enough ..."

I think maybe it's Jennifer, but she doesn't know about me being here.

Or does she?

I go outside to find out.

Yup, it's Jennifer outside Adult World. She's standing in the parking lot, away from the line of men waiting to get inside. When she sees me, she shakes her head and turns around to get back in her car.

"Shit ..." I chase after her, but before I reach her, she's

closed the car door and locked herself inside.

"Jennifer. Stop. Open the door."

She puts the key in the ignition. "No."

"I was going to tell you ..." I say as one of Adult World's regular customers, clearly oblivious to what's happening, passes and says hi to me. I nod in response, mostly so he'll just keep moving and I can finish my sentence. "... but I knew this is how you'd react. You'd think I was some kind of, y'know ..." I lower my voice so the customers can't hear. "*Perv* or something. Isn't that what you said that time we drove past it?"

"You said you'd never been here," she says. "You didn't know anything about it."

I laugh and say, "I still don't."

She's not laughing.

"Look ... Mike's dad owns the place. He offered me the job, the money was good, so ..."

She makes a disgusted face. "I should have known. You're just as bad as he is."

"What? No. Besides, he's not that bad."

She makes another face, as if she knows something I don't.

"What?"

"Nothing," she says. "So I guess this is why you always want to ... where you pick up all your little ... toys."

"No. That's not why. I do it because, y'know, I like to ..." I know there's a line of men around who probably wouldn't understand or who might make fun of me, so I lower my voice when I finish with, "... be with you. I ... I love you."

I'm surprised how easily the words come out. Sure, I'd thought it, but I had no intention of saying it - not yet, anyway. I guess tough times call for strong measures.

It obviously works, because she seems to melt a little.

But she shakes it off right away, as if remembering where we are and what's going on. She smirks like she doesn't believe my declaration of love.

I think about the redhead that came in way back on my second day at Adult World and how the fact that Tommy worked there seemed to be a deal breaker for her - or for her friend, at least ... which is odd, considering *she* was the one buying the vibrator.

"Look, can I at least get in the car?" I plead.

"No. I don't want you touching anything - or me. Who knows where your hands have been? Who knows what else goes on around here?"

"Jennifer, I'm only here for the money."

Robby yells, "Hey, Brian. You gonna be long?" from the doorway of the store.

"I'll be there in a minute!" I say without looking.

"Okay, 'cause she's almost here and ... Hey, is that your girlfriend ... Jenny? Hi, I'm -"

"Just go the fuck back inside, Robby!"

I don't look, but I can tell he's thrown by my anger. Truth is, so am I. And so is Jennifer.

I step back from the car to calm myself and as I do I notice a limousine arrive.

"You lied to me," Jennifer says.

"Well, I didn't exactly lie, per se." Again with the *per se*. I make a vow that it's the last time I'll ever use it in a sentence.

"You let me think one thing while another was the truth," she says. "You lied."

"I needed money, I took a job. I don't have parents to pay my way, like you. I wish I did. But I don't. I have to do it all on my own. This was the best way available to me right now."

The men in line hoot and holler and for a second I

believe it's in support of me and the rather weak stand I've taken. But they're looking at Holly Silva, who steps out of the limousine and is led toward the store by a rather large man who I assume is either her driver, bodyguard, or boyfriend - or all of the above.

She's dressed in a shiny gown and looks very made-up. Typical porn actress sense of style.

For some reason she looks at me at the same time I look at her and I think I detect a bit of a smile as she enters the store. But she probably smiles at everybody.

I acknowledge her in as subtle a way possible and say, "Shit," as I turn back to Jennifer. "I gotta go back to work." I look at her apologetically. "Can we talk about this later?"

"I won't be around later," she says in a huff as she starts the car.

"Where you gonna be?"

"Out - maybe with somebody who's not a *liar.*"

She sounds really childish, so I react in the same way. "Maybe Rick Schmidt's available."

"Maybe he is."

"You know you haven't exactly told me the truth all the time," I say. I don't know why. It's not like I know for sure she's ever lied to me about Rick. But I take a shot.

"What's that supposed to mean?"

"You know."

I must be wrong, because she shakes her head, puts the car in gear, and drives off.

I curse Mike for putting the idea of her and Rick in my head in the first place, then try to forget about the whole thing as I go back inside to work.

Of course, it's impossible, though. I may be losing Jennifer, the love of my life. It seems that way, anyway, and it makes me feel hollow inside.

I want to leave work and follow her, but know I can't, so I fight the discomfort until I can deal with it - and Jennifer - later.

As I reenter Adult World, Robby makes a whipping motion with his hand, followed by a loud, "Wa-psh."

I've had enough of him today - and in general. "Shut the fuck up," I snap.

I'm either too loud or too intense about it, because everyone in the store, including Holly, freezes. I make an apologetic face to her and she smiles back as I go to work like nothing happened. Thankfully, everyone's attention quickly returns to the signing.

During the next two hours, Holly seems to look at me a lot. But, again, that must be what makes her so successful; she probably makes every guy in the place think he's the one she's looking at.

She poses for photographs with most every customer and either signs the products they buy or kisses the packaging to leave a dark red lipstick imprint of her mouth on them. As a result, the store sells a ton of videos and, surprisingly, almost all its stock of the rubber mold of "her" that she's there to promote in the first place.

Like Robby said, they're selling like hotcakes, and even though I'm witnessing it happen, it's hard for me to believe that there are guys actually buying a rubber mold of a woman's vagina - from the woman herself! On top of that, they seem comfortable with it, which is even more incredible, considering everyone knows what they're gonna do with the thing once they get it home.

I cringe just thinking about them all violating this

inanimate object and somehow getting off on it. It kind of reminds me of the poor little monkey and the mother-shaped carpet I saw in the film during Mr. McCoy's Social Studies class back on my birthday - only this is something entirely more disgusting.

Every time I say my standard, "Come again," I also think, *And don't forget to wipe it off when you're finished.* Once I even say it, by accident.

The customer I say it to doesn't seem to believe he heard me right, but Tommy does and he cracks up when the customer's gone.

I don't think he expected me to say something like that, to get down to the level that's pretty much the norm in Adult World. But something about the anger I feel for the situation with Jennifer seems to bring it out of me. Or maybe the store just brings it out of people. Or maybe it's a combination of the two.

Part of my anger is reserved for Mike. I've begun to think he must be the one who told Jennifer that I work here. After all, who else knows? My mom is the only other person I can think of who might have contact with Jennifer ... and I *know* she wouldn't say anything.

So when Mike shows up at the store, I cut him off before he heads toward Holly.

"What are you doing?" he says, "I wanna meet -"

I grab his arm and escort him to the back room. "Did you tell anybody I work here?"

"No."

I look at him suspiciously. "Really? Not even Tracy, maybe?"

"I don't think so. Why?"

"'Cause she showed up here."

"Who? Tracy?"

"No. Why the fuck would I care if Tracy came in? I'm

talking about Jennifer."

Mike cringes. "Ooh."

"Exactly." I take another moment to figure out how she could have known. "How about at your party?"

Mike shakes his head, then seems to remember something. His face crinkles with remorse. "I don't think so," he says, which pretty much means yes. That must be it.

"Shit," I say as I remember that Rick Schmidt was there. Maybe in his drunken state Mike told Rick, or maybe Rick overheard Mike tell someone else. Either way, it somehow got to Jennifer. But none of that matters now.

"Sorry, Bro," he says weakly. "Seriously. I hope I didn't screw up your game."

"Ah, it's my own fault," I say. And it is. I should have told her from the beginning.

I let Mike go out front to meet Holly as I stay back and call Jennifer. She doesn't answer and I hang up on her voicemail.

Damn.

I call Jennifer a few more times over the next half hour, but she never answers. The last time I call, I'm in the back room alone and it sounds like Holly's finished with the signing because I hear her coming back.

"Is it okay if I change back there?" she says.

I hear Mr. Welch say, "Yes. Use the room off to the left."

Then Mike says, "I'll show you."

"I think I can figure it out," Holly says before entering

the room I'm in just as I hang up on Jennifer's voicemail for probably the tenth time. I glare at the phone and fight my urge to punch it.

Holly closes the door and looks like she's about to change her clothing.

So I turn to leave. "Sorry. I'll -"

"Don't let me kick you out," she says. I figure she probably isn't self-conscious about letting a stranger see her change. Hundreds of thousands, if not millions, have seen her do much worse.

"It's okay," I say. "I'm done."

"You all right?"

"Fine." I continue to the door, but when I push, it won't open. I make sure to turn the knob and push again. Nothing. On my third try, I can hear Robby laugh outside.

I look at Holly and say, "I'm sorry. They're children!" loud enough so Robby can hear.

Holly doesn't seem to care. "It's okay. I'm used to it."

"Mind if I wait it out a minute?"

"No," she says. "Grab a seat."

I sit in a chair far away from her and look in the other direction, so she can change. But she doesn't seem to be in a hurry. I look at my phone again to appear otherwise occupied.

"So, who was that you were trying to call?" she asks. "Girlfriend?"

"Yeah." I accidentally turn and look at her, but she hasn't started changing yet. She's smiling.

"What?" I say.

"It's nice you said yes. Most guys wouldn't. Afraid it'll ruin their shot or something. Like I'm gonna do any guy off the street in Bumfuck, New Jersey."

"Pennsylvania," I say.

"Right," she says. "Sorry."

"And it's pronounced Bum-*fook*," I say, kidding, then look away again so she can change. But it doesn't sound like she is.

She laughs and continues, "Some girls would, though. Some'd go down on all of you, thinking it gets them something … or just 'cause they like it."

"Yeah, I've seen it … I think," I say. "I mean, I personally haven't …"

"Right … girlfriend."

I nod and indicate the guys out front. "I think they think I'll … or that you'll …"

"So … what should we tell them?"

"Huh?" I say as I try the door again. No luck. "Oh, um, nothing. The truth."

"Sometimes a lie's the better way to go."

"Heh. I don't know about that. Besides, I don't want to give them the idea you … y'know."

"Eh, let 'em have their idea," she says. "That's all it is. Won't hurt anybody."

I consider this as I listen and hear what sounds like Robby being called away by Mr. Welch. I try the door again and this time it opens. So I head out.

"So, Brian," Holly says, stopping me. "It is 'Brian', right?" I turn and nod. "Where can a girl go to grab a bite around here?"

I think about it, but can't come up with anything in particular. "Um, there's a buncha places. What are you hungry for?"

A sexy smile curls her lips. I'm still not convinced it means anything. She's just in that mode, like everybody else in this business.

I run through a couple of nearby restaurants for her. I don't know many, though. It's not like I eat out a lot. I do know of one new place that's supposed to be kind of nice. I saw a review of it in the newspaper back when I was looking for a car.

I tell her about it and it seems to be exactly what she's looking for. She follows me out without having changed any of her clothing.

"Brian's taking me out for a bite," she announces to the store, but mostly to Mr. Welch.

"He is?" Mr. Welch says with what looks like a combination of surprise, doubt, and perhaps pride. I have the same look on my face, I think.

I am?

"That's okay, isn't it?" she says.

I'm too stunned to answer, but it doesn't matter, because she wasn't talking to me.

Mr. Welch nods. Mike's jaw drops as Holly leads me to the door. I follow, confused.

As we go, she whispers to them all, "He's got the most beautiful cock I've ever seen."

"No he doesn't," Mike says. Everyone looks at him. "What? I grew up with him."

I shrug helplessly and look apologetic - I know Mike had his heart set on getting to know her - as she pulls me out of the store.

In the limousine, I look away as Holly changes her clothing and tones down her makeup.

"You didn't have to say that to them," I say.

"I know. But it was fun to see their faces, wasn't it? You're gonna have quite the reputation come tomorrow."

I laugh at the idea, then think about Jennifer again.

Holly can probably tell what's on my mind. "You wanna try again?"

"Hm?"

"The phone."

"Oh. Um, no. That's okay. She's not going to answer."

"Okay," she says. "I'm finished. You can look now."

I turn to look back at Holly and am immediately struck by how different she looks, now that she's out of her makeup and porn star wardrobe. She's very pretty and looks maybe ten years younger than I thought she was with the getup on. It's like she's a whole different person. Most people would probably find this person less desirable than the other, but I'm not one of them. I think she's much prettier this way.

But it's not like I'm going to do anything about it; not while I'm in my relationship with Jennifer - which may or may not be over at this point. I don't want to consider the fact that it might be finished, though, so until Jennifer calms down - which I hope she does - and talks to me, this is a nice distraction. And I'm kind of curious to find out what kind of person does what Holly does.

Outside of the restaurant that I recommended, the bodyguard/driver - who, it turns out, is not her boyfriend - lets Holly and me out of the limousine. He follows us to the restaurant until Holly stops him.

"It's okay," she says. "You can wait in the car. I'll be fine."

"You sure?" he says, then looks at me.

I can't help laughing. *Do I look even remotely like a threat?*

She nods that it's okay and he lets us approach the restaurant, which apparently on Saturday nights becomes more like a nightclub. In preparation, there's a bouncer working the door to check I.D.'s.

"I don't have I-D," I say out of the side of my mouth.

"Neither do I," Holly says. "Just keep walking."

She smiles at the bouncer, who opens the door for us. He barely looks at me, he's so struck by her.

I have to agree with Robby; she definitely has some kind of star quality.

Inside the restaurant, Holly and I are seated in a booth and she immediately orders a shaker of vodka martinis. "Very dry," she stresses to the waiter.

She sits back in the booth, spreads her arms out, and looks around the place. I do the same. It's very nice and surprisingly hip, considering the norm in the area. A deejay's setting up his board by a small dance-floor area.

"Oh, good. There'll be music," Holly says and looks back at me. "This is nice. Good choice."

I nod thanks you.

When the waiter returns with the martinis, he pours two drinks.

I'm not much of a drinker, like I said, but figure, *What the hell; I'm in a bar. My girlfriend's dumping me. And I'm not driving. Why not drink?*

So I do.

I try to keep up with Holly, but she's clearly much more comfortable with almost straight vodka than I am. She barely reacts to the taste of the alcohol, while I, on the other hand, wince eating a vodka-soaked olive.

Soon, the place is filled with people, the deejay is playing music, and by the third shaker of martinis, I've given up trying to keep up with Holly. I'm plenty drunk already.

My inhibitions, such as they are, are way down and Holly can no doubt see that I'm thinking something as I stare at her.

"What?" she says.

I'm not thinking about sex. Honest. What I'm thinking is that she's a lot different than I expected her to be and I say so.

She looks offended. "What's that supposed to mean?"

"No, no. I mean … well, I've seen some of the people that have come through … I just mean … you're a lot prettier than … I expected." I hope I'm remotely clear about what I'm saying. I can't tell, as drunk as I am.

"Oh," she says. "Thank you."

"You even look different from inside the store. Must be that green fluorescent light. It's awful. Washes everything out, makes your skin look green. I mean, not *yours* … everybody's. It's bad, bad lighting," I say, slurring.

She laughs and looks at me curiously. "What are you, a photographer or something?"

"No. A painter. Well, I'm going to be … that is, next year I -"

"Really? What do you paint?"

"The usual. Still life, landscape, people …"

"Wow," she says. "That's impressive." She looks at me like she's genuinely impressed and not just saying it. "Kinda sexy, too," she adds with a smile. "Do me."

I'm not sure what she means and no doubt look puzzled, although I can't feel all of my facial muscles.

"Do me … right here."

I run through the possibilities of what she could mean. *Is she talking about sex?*

She must realize what she's saying and clarifies with a laugh. "I mean draw me."

"Oh," I say, a little embarrassed. "Uh, sure. I could ... I guess."

She hands me a pen from her purse, then one of the white cloth napkins on the table. "Do it on this."

I nod, even though it's an unconventional medium to work with, and she poses for me.

I take a moment to survey her face, trying to look as professional and painterly as possible, then begin to draw what I see.

She seems self-conscious as I examine the lines of her eyes, nose, and mouth and copy them as best I can on the napkin. It's as if she thinks I'm peering into her soul or something, like I might see something she doesn't want me to see. I kind of like it. For the first time I feel like we're even close to being on the same level.

"Can I ask you a question?" I say.

"That *is* a question."

"Another one, then."

She stops posing and stares at me, apparently disappointed. "As long as it's not *the* question: How did I end up doing this ..."

"No. Actually, I was going to ask you how old you are?"

She goes back to posing. "Don't you know you should never ask a girl her age?"

"I know ... It's just that ... you seem so young. I mean, in a good way ... pretty."

"Good save."

"It's true."

She smiles and I can see she's letting down her guard now that she's spent some time with me. It gives her a pleasant softness that I try to catch in the portrait - but it's difficult, given the medium and the fact that I'm drunk.

"I'm nineteen," she says.

I don't quite believe her. "You're only a year older than I am?"

She stares at me, I guess while she decides if she can trust me enough to tell me a secret, then takes out her wallet and shows me her driver's license. I confirm her age, then notice her name is different. "'Elizabeth Jensen'?" I ask.

"Beth. Yes."

"Heh. Nice to meet you, Beth Jensen," I say with a formal, yet drunken, nod.

She nods in return.

I continue to draw for another minute or so and consider the other question. As pretty as she is, I can't help wondering why she isn't a "real" actress.

"So," I say, "what if I did ask you *the* question ... would you answer?"

She seems bothered. "Why does everybody want to know that?"

"Well, because what you, um, do is a little ... unusual. Don't you think?"

"I'm just an actress," she says. "There're lots of actresses out there."

"It's a little different, isn't it?"

"Why?" she says. "'Legit' actresses - act*ors*, too - sleep with people all the time ... and that's only *to get* jobs. I'm just not a hypocrite about it. I am what I am. You like it, fine; you don't, I don't care. I wasn't raped as a kid. I'm not a drug addict. I just don't think there's anything wrong with sex. Somebody wants to film me? So what? I give 'em a little of my body, my looks, while I still have them, and I get a lot of money in return. It's not like I'm giving them my soul. I have a choice in what I do. I decide."

I accept her answer, although I don't completely

believe it all, and go back to drawing.

"So … Brian," she says and adjusts herself in her seat, "Have you ever seen any of my movies?"

"I'd be lying if I said I hadn't."

"And what's the difference between watching it and doing it on film?"

"Well …" I say, but don't continue. I figure it's pretty obvious.

"If you buy it, watch it, get off on it, you can't judge it," she says.

Maybe she has a point.

"Nobody's a saint, Brian. Nobody's a sinner, either. We all sell ourselves to get what we want. Even artists."

There's definitely some truth to that, as I'm beginning to learn. But I don't want to talk about it anymore, so I remain silent while I finish the image of her.

I check the two-dimensional Holly - or Beth, rather - against the three-dimensional Beth in front of me one last time before handing the napkin to her.

She looks at the portrait and seems more impressed by me. "Wow. You're really good. I thought it would be like one of those cheesy things the guys at carnivals do. But … Wow."

I take the compliment humbly, but love to hear it. Any kind of encouragement is always welcome. And it doesn't get much better than "Wow."

She not only seems to think it's good, but also appears genuinely affected by it. She even gets kind of emotional.

When she looks at me, it's as if the last of her guard goes down before my eyes. "Nobody's ever drawn me before …" she says.

I don't think it's that nobody's ever drawn her before; I think maybe it's that I made her look soft, gentle, graceful even, and maybe nobody's ever seen her in that kind of light before - including herself … and maybe that's the reason she does what she does. But what do I know?

"Yeah, I don't normally draw …" I was about to say I don't normally draw portraits, but am interrupted by thoughts of Jennifer. She had a similar reaction to the drawing I made of her on my birthday.

It was that reaction - which was the first time I really tried to sketch a face and capture the essence of someone - that set the tone for our relationship.

I feel guilty for having drawn this girl I just met in the same way. No doubt Beth can see the change in my expression as I think about it.

"What?" she says.

"Nothing." I excuse myself to call Jennifer again. As I stand, I can feel how wobbly drunk I am. "Whoa."

Beth grabs my arm as I steady myself. I nod thanks, then stumble to the men's room and dial Jennifer's number.

A man answers this time. "Hello," is all he says. I don't know who it is and although it may very well be a wrong number, in my foggy head all I can see is Rick Schmidt answering her phone for her. And in this vision, they're naked.

Instead of waiting to find out if either scenario is true, I hang up without saying a word. I put the phone in my pocket without checking the number and head back out to the restaurant.

When I return to the table, Beth is gone. For a while I think she's ditched me, until I see her out by the dance floor with two men who are talking to - and leering at - her.

I figure she's busy and remain in the booth to savor the moment of down time. But after watching Beth talk to the two men a bit, I can see that they're getting a little hands-y and figure I should probably get up and see if she's okay.

So I do.

As I arrive, I hear one of the men ask her if she's alone.

Apparently pleased by my return, Beth says, "No. I'm with him." She takes my arm, pulls me further onto the dance floor, and starts to dance.

"So ... did she answer?" she asks as she swivels her hips like a cobra before a snake charmer.

"No. And I should probably go."

"No. Stay. Have fun." She dances closer to me. 'Holly' seems to be back. "Don't worry. She'll forgive you. Look at you ..." She squeezes my cheeks and smiles. "Who wouldn't want to just eat you alive?"

I'm embarrassed - not only at the compliment, but at the flirting she's doing with me.

Holly is *definitely* back.

I consider how much of that is due to the alcohol.

She moves close, like she's going to kiss me, but pulls away at the last millisecond, smiles as if she knows something I don't, and begins to bump and grind in a way that would drive any man crazy. I'm certainly not immune - especially after a few martinis - and end up dancing along with her in a way I've never danced in my life. I haven't even danced like this with Jennifer.

I get so carried away that I don't even care about all the people staring at the two of us. But that might just be an effect of the alcohol.

After five minutes of this, she moves in close and

kisses me. And I let her. I suppose I'm driven by the thought of Jennifer with someone else. But also, I have to admit that kissing Holly turns me on a lot more than I expected it would. I'm ashamed to say how much, but there's definitely a pup tent raised at my crotch.

So between that and the drunkenness, I don't resist too much when a half-hour later Holly leads me out of the restaurant and back to the limousine.

In the limo, I go along with Holly's come-on further and we quickly start to run the bases.

I get to second standing up and wonder about moving on to third when I'm cut off by her saying, "Bite me."

"Huh?"

"Bite me."

I'm still not sure what she means. "Where?"

"Wherever you want."

I go along and nip at her neck, then shoulder.

"No," she says. "Harder … like this." She bites me on the neck - and I mean *bites*. It's really hard. And it hurts.

I flinch in pain and wonder if she removed skin.

I'm not sure what to do next. It clearly turns her on, though. Why it would, I have no idea.

She continues to sink her teeth into me in several places, from my cheek down to my stomach. I fight the pain as long as I can, but she's biting way too hard.

"Ow!" I say and finally have to pull away.

"What? Don't you like that?"

"Um … actually, no."

She puts her hand on my crotch and can definitely feel that I'm turned on. "Sure you do. I can tell."

Before I can explain that it's just residual arousal from before and that, if anything, her gnawing has turned me off, she proceeds to unzip my pants and put her hand on me. The physical pleasure returns immediately.

Still, the biting has snapped me out of my trance just long enough to realize where I am and what's happening. "I really shouldn't. I have a ... girlfriend."

"No one else has to know," she whispers in my ear with hot breath, which only turns me on more.

She presses hard against me and grinds her hips against mine in hypnotic rhythm. I like it. A lot.

Then she bites me again.

Even though, so far, this is definitely the craziest thing to ever happen to me and I'd love to tell the rest of the story, I'd rather not go into what happens next - mostly because I can't win in either scenario. If I say I stopped Holly because I didn't want to ruin what I might still have with Jennifer and that the whole thing, with the biting and all, was just too bizarre for me, guys'll think I'm an idiot. And if I say I had amazing, white-hot, monkey sex with her then and there in the limo, girls'll think I'm a jerk. Either way, I lose.

So when I stumble out of the limousine in the parking lot of Adult World a little later, I vow to never tell a soul exactly what happened.

Besides, like with most things, no matter what I say, people are gonna believe what they want to. So it doesn't really matter one way or the other.

I'm probably not legally sober yet when I'm dropped off by Holly, but am nevertheless pretty clear-headed, if a bit queasy, after the experience and anxious to get home. Also, Adult World is still open, as it is at all hours on weekends, and I want to get out of there before someone spots me.

So I slither over to my car, start it, and drive with caution out of the parking lot and toward home.

Thankfully, I arrive at my house safely.

I sneak inside, go right into the bathroom, strip, and step into the shower, where I close my eyes and revel in the feel of warm, clean water hitting my face.

Sadly, the soothing sensation doesn't last long, because soon it feels like the room is spinning. I open my eyes to steady myself against the tile wall and stop the rising nausea in my stomach, but it's too late. Over the next fifteen minutes, I puke my guts out. In fact, my stomach's *still* trying to empty itself even after everything's already out. It's awful - but a hell of an ab workout.

When my stomach finally gives up - or is worn out - I brush my teeth, stagger into the bedroom, and collapse in a heap on my bed.

SEVENTH

I could have used at least a good twelve hours of sleep to recover from my night with Holly, but the next morning I'm rudely awakened by Mike slapping at my leg.

"Wake up, Bro. Up an' at 'em."

I'm a mess. There's a coat of what feels like shellac in my mouth and my head's throbbing from dehydration.

"Damn. You look like hell," Mike says.

"Thanks."

The last thing I want to do is get up, but Mike forces me to. I have no idea why and don't have the mental clarity to ask him.

"So," Mike prods, "what happened last night?"

"Nothing," I say. "Nothing happened." I'm not going to tell him, either way. I will never tell anyone.

"Sure," Mike says. "Right. You went out with a porn star and nothing happened."

I nod.

"I think that hickey on your neck ... and the one on your cheek ... would beg to differ."

"'Hickey'?" I hop to the mirror and look. Sure enough,

there are marks on my body. Bite marks. "Shit."

"You still stickin' with your story?"

"They're not hickeys," I say. "She bit me."

Mike nods in approval. "Niiiiice."

"It wasn't nice. It fucking hurt. She was trying to eat me or something."

"And you didn't want her to?!"

"Not the good kind of eat," I say. "I mean, *eat*. I think she removed flesh."

"Ooh, and she was kinky. I hate you."

"I'm telling you, it was beyond that. It was *weird*." I turn my back to the mirror. There's a mark there, too. "Aw, man. Look at that."

Mike laughs.

"It's not funny," I say.

"To me it is."

I'm finally clear enough to ask Mike what the hell he's doing in my room, waking me up, anyway.

"My dad tried to call you. You were supp -" he starts to say.

I don't need him to finish; I was supposed to be at work an hour ago.

I look at my phone to check the time and see that the battery is dead - probably from all the trying to call Jennifer last night.

"Oh, shit!"

I jump up, get dressed, grab the phone charger, force myself to eat two Pop-Tarts through the residual nausea I feel, and drive myself to work.

Mike follows me in his car. He probably wants to see what's going to happen to me - or, more specifically, how his dad will treat me after this.

Tommy and Robby are at Adult World already and their applause sounds like the thunder of a kettledrum as I enter. I do my best to brush it off. The last thing I want is any more attention drawn to the whole episode. I just want to forget about it. I want everybody else to forget about it, too.

So I say nothing when Tommy asks me about what happened. "She, uh … ?" he says. He doesn't have to say it; he knows I know what he means.

I barely acknowledge the question.

"C'mon," he says. "I got twenty bucks ridin' on this. Robby said Holly would. I said she wouldn't. Which is it?"

"I'll bet she gave Brian Holly *wood.*"

They all laugh. I don't. For some reason I feel kind of defensive about her. She's a person, after all. A little odd, maybe, but still a person.

I can't say anything, though. Any bit of information will only encourage them to prod further.

"Tell us, Brian," Robby says. "She have a Holly bush - or was it more of a Holly wreath? You know, just a ring around the rosy."

I try to ignore their antics, but it's hard. Thankfully Mr. Welch comes out from the back to interrupt them.

"Sorry I'm late, Mr. Welch," I say.

"He has a pretty good excuse, don't you think, Boss?" Robby says.

Mike chimes in. "He says nothing happened."

Mr. Welch nods and winks at me. "Always the best way to play it."

"I'm not playing. I have a girlfriend. At least I think I

still do …"

"Was she there?" Mr. Welch asks.

"What? No."

He shrugs. "So what are you so worried about? Rule Number One: Nobody sees you, you didn't do it." He smiles and winks again.

I'm not sure if he's kidding, but still wonder if maybe he's right. I'm not sure. I've never been in this kind of situation before. But Mr. Welch is an adult and probably has, so I figure he must know something I don't.

Still, I don't want to lie anymore to Jennifer.

But I don't want the relationship to end, either - and it definitely would if she found out.

I consider that maybe I've put the cart before the horse here. I still haven't gotten past the whole "I work at Adult World" issue with her. I may never get past it. And if that's the case, none of this matters.

I need to find out if there's even a relationship left before I can decide what to do. It's the not knowing that makes you crazy with this kind of thing.

That night, after work, I use my mother's makeup to hide the bite marks on my cheek and neck and drive over to Jennifer's house. Since she still won't answer her phone, I decide I'll just go see her in person.

On the Kinney's doorstep I dial Jennifer's phone one more time. I figure if I can hear it ring, I'll know she's inside. I think I do, so I hang up and press the doorbell.

Mr. Kinney answers. I wonder if she told him about me working at Adult World, but figure it doesn't much matter. Even if she did tell him, he can't really pass judgment on me, being a customer and all.

It doesn't look like he knows, but I can tell from his tone that he knows *something's* up.

"Hi, Mr. Kinney. Is Jennifer here?"

"No."

"You sure?" I say, "'Cause I just heard her phone ring inside -"

"Well," he says, "I guess she forgot to -"

The door opens wider and Jennifer appears. She looks at her father, who shrugs an apology - I guess for so clearly lying to me - and leaves Jennifer alone with me.

"What do you want?"

"I want to talk to you," I say.

"Why?"

"What do you mean, 'why'? I ..." I stumble for the right words, but in the end the only right ones, which I say, are, "Look, I'm sorry I didn't tell you about where I work. I really am. But, I've got college and, well, there's the prom - if you still want to go ..."

"Don't say that."

"What? The prom?"

"No," she says. "'I'm sorry ... *but.*' I hate that. Are you sorry or aren't you?"

"Of course I am," I say and let my body go limp with regret.

"Well," she says, "I am too."

I freeze, totally thrown by this unexpected turn. I want to rattle my head comically, like a confused cartoon character, but manage to maintain my cool. "What do you have to be sorry for?"

"I know you need money ..."

Heh, I think, a little strengthened now. *Maybe that point I made in the parking lot sank in ... eventually.*

"And I was just ... I guess I wasn't thinking about

that."

I stare and wait for her to continue. I figure it's better to just shut up in situations like this.

"I'm just … I was afraid that, well, you're going to be graduating soon and you're going away and I'm scared about you leaving."

I smile. It's nice to hear. Maybe she really does care about me as much I care about her.

I try to put her mind at ease and perhaps make the fact that I'll be leaving less of an issue by saying, "Trust me, not half as scared as I am."

Then, to tie it back to Adult World and make sure it's not an issue anymore, I add, "Hell, I may not even be able to at this point. If I don't make enough money, I'm not going anywhere. I'm starting to think I should just go to business school - something practical." And the truth is, I am kind of thinking about it these days.

"You don't want to do that," she says. "That's not you."

"How do you know?"

The last of yesterday's chill seems to vanish and she looks at me with that warm, glowing smile that makes me so weak. "Because I know you."

I smile back. "Well, I wish I was still a junior. I could use the extra year."

"But then you wouldn't be able to take me to the Senior Prom next week."

"You still want to go?"

She smiles.

"Really?" I ask.

"Don't you want me to?"

"No. I mean, yeah. Of course."

"You did say you loved me yesterday."

I did?

I try to replay the tape in my head. *Oh, right. Outside Adult World.*

While I didn't exactly say it under the best of circumstances, just because I was under duress doesn't mean it's still not true. It is. And I know it is. She has to know it, too.

"Did you mean it? Or were you just trying to win me over?"

"A little of both," I say with a coy smile. "Well, a *lot* of both."

I know I haven't really answered her question. And even though I said it already yesterday, it's a little different now. Hell, it's a *lot* is different. Plus, it's not the easiest thing to say - especially when it's the first time you'll ever say it for real.

I mean, yeah, I've said it to my ... actually, come to think of it, I don't think I've ever said it to anybody - not even my mom. Of course, I do love her, but why haven't I said it? And why hasn't she said it to me? Is that normal?

Hmmm ...

Jennifer continues to look at me, waiting for my answer. I snap my thoughts back to the moment at hand, stare at her another few seconds to make sure I'm doing the right thing, and say, "I meant it," with as much gravity as I can muster.

The next moment after that, as I wait for her to respond, is an eternity. She's just staring at me, her face blank.

Has time stopped or something?

Finally, I see her lips stretch across her face, so I can tell time is indeed moving, but it still must be going very, very slowly.

The corners of her mouth curl into a broad smile and a glint forms in her eyes. It's the prettiest I've ever seen her and now I'm kind of glad time has slowed down so I can enjoy the moment.

"I love you, too," she says and everything returns to regular speed, but somehow calmer and strangely brighter than it had been only moments before.

She moves forward to kiss me and I meet her halfway. It's a really good kiss. I even hear her sigh during it. Or maybe it's me. Whoever it is, I don't care. As long as we're back together.

It's great.

Only now I have the other hurdle to deal with: whether to tell her about my experience with Holly.

I'm still not sure. And when I'm not sure, I find it best to wait. And in the waiting, I hope the answer will come.

Still, I can't shake the nagging questions about what Jennifer did the night I was with Holly. That alone is reason enough not to let her know - at least that's what I tell myself. I know it's a terrible justification, but I'm reaching out for any straw I can grasp at this point.

While I figure all this out, I also plan for the prom - and, more importantly, afterward. I don't know if Jennifer still wants to have sex with me and I'm afraid to ask.

Like everything else, I'll just have to wait and see.

At Adult World the day after I make up with Jennifer, Tommy works with me while Mike and Robby hang out. It's kind of quiet, so we play "baseball" using a dildo as a bat and a small, vibrating sphere as the ball.

While we play, Mike asks me about the prom because he wants to get a limousine and make a big to-do out of it all. I tell him that, yes, I'm still going with Jennifer.

"So it's on, then," he says. "You'll actually crack that nut ... and bust your own in the process." He swings and hits the ball. "Probably won't take long, you being such a rookie and all."

I hadn't really thought about that ... until now. *Great.*

Tommy fields the ball and tags Mike at "first base," the center of the Asian video section. "Don't listen to him, Brian. It's like riding a bicycle. You've ridden a bicycle before, haven't you?"

I step up to bat and shrug.

"He'll probably last, like, two seconds," Mike says. I get the feeling he's still bitter about me keeping him on the on-deck circle with Holly, so I give him the free shot and nod in agreement before striking out.

"You know what I do sometimes?" Robby says as I hand Tommy the rubber bat and take the ball to pitch to him. "If you start out and you have to piss and you hold it ... it's kinda like doing a Suicide Squeeze, like it pinches off your vast difference or something ... and you last longer."

Tommy misses my pitch and squints at Robby. "Pinches off your *what?*"

"Your *vast difference*," Robby says. "What the jiz comes out of. You know, the tube."

Tommy drops the bat and can't seem to believe what he just heard. "What are you, twelve? It's the 'vas deferens' ... not 'vast difference'."

Robby looks at me. I nod in agreement. We learned this two years ago in Sex Ed. He looks at Mike, who nods, too. "I thought it was 'vast difference'."

Tommy has stopped paying attention to the game. "Why would it be 'vast difference'?"

"Well," Robby says, "because it's like the difference

between the two tubes. One you piss out of, the other you, you know, you come out of. Big difference. Like your throat. You eat down one tube and you breathe down the other, but at one point it's the same pipe and there's that flap thing that goes back and forth, depending on what you're doing."

Tommy laughs. "Are your parents brother and sister?"

"Seriously, though," Robby says, addressing us all, as if imparting the wisdom of his experience, "If you have to piss, it's like the *vas deferens* ..." He turns to Tommy. "Is that okay, college boy?" Tommy smiles and nods. "It's like it's plugged up ... so it's harder to come."

Mike and I look at him. *Who knows? Maybe he's right.*

After all, Robby was right about the "little death" thing - sort of.

I looked it up and yes, *La petite mort* is actually a French idiom for orgasm, even though it refers more to the spiritual release that some believe accompanies it than the actual orgasm itself. I think there may be some truth in that notion - based on my experience.

Tommy shakes his head, picks up the bat, and looks at me as he steps to the plate. "Just pace yourself and change things up when it feels too good. You'll be fine." He settles in and mutters, "Vast difference," before getting a double off my pitch.

As Mike tosses the ball back to me, I hear the door open behind me.

Mike looks toward it with disbelief and says, "Jenny."

"Very funny," I say, then turn and see that it is, in fact, Jennifer entering the store.

I put the ball down and go to her as the game dissolves behind me.

"Hey. What're you doing?" I block as much of the store as I can from her view - especially the booth area.

She cranes her neck around me to sneak a peek. "I wanted to see where you work."

"Really? You sure?"

She nods and smiles a polite hello to Tommy and Robby. They nod back and look down as if addressing royalty. She's definitely out of place here.

Mike steps forward and hands me the ball to resume the game. "Uh, she shouldn't be in here." He looks at Tommy for confirmation.

But Tommy either doesn't care, or he doesn't want Mike to have his way, because he turns to me and says, "She okay, Brian?"

I make a doubtful face. "Well ..."

Tommy nods and goes back to the register. "Good enough for me."

Now that she has the go-ahead, Jennifer enters further. She and Mike share a look and he moves away.

I stay close by as she examines the store. She seems shocked, amused, maybe even turned on by the things she sees.

"Who buys this stuff?" she says.

"Heh. You'd be surprised." I try to hide the knowing look on my face. "Husbands, fathers. Women, too, even. It's not as weird as you'd think. Well, it's still a little weird ..."

She surveys more of the store, then picks up a bottle of edible massage oil and shows it to me. "I think I'm going to buy this." She looks around to make sure she can't be heard and adds, "For Saturday."

So it appears things truly are back to normal - for her, anyway. For me, there's still the dilemma over the Holly incident.

Days later, I'm still turning the Holly issue over and over in my brain as I wolf down dinner to get to work on time. I'm filling in for Robby, who's going to cover my weekend shifts so I can be free to enjoy the prom - and anything that might come after it - without having to worry about working the next day.

I finish dinner with a few minutes to spare before I need to head off to work and since it's one of the rare times these days when my mom is home and Gary isn't there, I decide to see what she thinks about the situation.

"Mom?"

"Yeah?" She looks at me and I wait long enough to both find the right words and let her know that I'm going to ask her something important. She sets her fork down and looks nervous to hear what I'm going to say.

"If you, say, kissed someone besides Gary ... would you say that's cheating?"

She looks relieved it's all I'm asking and says, "Sure," as if that's the answer I'm looking for. Or perhaps she wants me to think she's a very moral person - which I suppose all parents want.

She must see on my face that it is indeed *not* the answer I'm looking for, though, because she adds, "Of course, I guess it depends on the type of kiss we're talking about ..."

I stare at her stone-faced and say, "A *kiss*."

She scrunches her face. I can tell she wants to say that it's okay, but just can't do it.

I know the right answer to that, though; I've always known. I didn't need her to confirm it. The main issue, however, is murkier.

"Would you tell him?" I ask.

She takes a breath and seems to go back and forth on the issue in her mind. "That's a tough call. It's not really a black and white ... I assume this is about you?"

I nod, although it's the last thing I want to admit.

"Well," she says, "What do *you* think you should do?"

"I dunno," I say with an uncomfortable laugh. "That's why I'm asking you."

She thinks about it some more. "Would you be telling her to make yourself feel better, or her?"

I'm not sure what the answer to that is - or even exactly what she means.

"I think a lot of times people come clean about something like that not so much because it's best for the relationship, but because they want to ease their own conscience," she says. "Like religious people who go to confession all the time. They behave badly, purge themselves, then go back and do it all over again."

I nod as I consider the notion. I'm still not sure of the answer.

"Let's put it this way," she says. "You gonna do it again?"

I won't ever see Holly again, that's for sure. So I can answer with a certain level of confidence. I shake my head.

"Then wouldn't it be better to just go forward and be a better person," she says, "a better boyfriend?"

I see her point. It's a good one - and makes me feel better about the possibility of not telling Jennifer, which is the last thing I want to do. I smile, nod, and head toward the door.

"It was just a kiss ... right?"

I turn back to see her look at me like a smiling prosecutor. I consider how to best answer and decide to just nod. That's the answer she wants to hear anyway. That's the answer that will cause her the least worry - and me the least judgment.

Clearly the Holly situation isn't settled for me, because I continue to consider my options as I work alone at Adult World and only get a break from it when a more immediate predicament presents itself. About an hour into my shift I hear the front door open and look up to see none other than Mr. Kinney enter again.

I instinctively duck behind the counter and, like before, watch the security monitor as he shops. This time, since I'm by myself, I don't know how I can possibly get out of him seeing me. All I can hope for is that he doesn't find anything to buy and leaves without coming to the register. But when he begins picking up items I know I'm screwed.

I run through all the things I can say to him and drive myself crazy trying to come up with the right words, until I realize it doesn't matter if he sees me anymore.

Jennifer already knows, so who cares what he thinks?

Maybe he'll hold it against me, but isn't what I have on him an even bigger thing? He can't judge me, lest he be judged himself. Isn't that what the good book - his good book - says?

I imagine all the possible scenarios to make sure I don't miss an angle that could come back to bite me in the ass, but can't think of any. So I smile to myself, stand back up, and wait by the register for him to come to me.

After he shops a few minutes without taking note of my presence, he approaches the register. "Um, did you get this month's - ?" he begins to say, but clams up when he sees me. It's almost comic, the look on his face.

"Hi, Mr. Kinney," I say.

"Brian. Uh, hi ... how are you?" he says, either out of reflex, or in an attempt to make his presence - and mine - seem normal.

"I'm fine. You?"

He looks around like he's on some kind of practical joke show and being filmed as we speak. "You, uh, you work here?"

I nod and point to my staff shirt.

"Does Jennifer - ?"

"Yes," I say to cut him off. "She knows." I don't want him to think for an instant he's got something on me. This is my moment; I will not let him take it from me ... after all those speeches he's given me.

Hah.

"Of course, she didn't like it ... but she knows it's just a job, so ..."

"Oh." He fumbles, as if trying to regain some of the usual advantage he has over me. "Well, then, um, maybe you can help me. I'm, uh, looking for some things for a, um, bachelor party and well, I don't really know what there is and ... Have you been here long?"

I love watching him squirm. "A few months now," I say with emphasis, to include all that implies.

Double-hah.

Then for laughs I press further. "Is there something specific you're looking for?"

"Uh," he says. "Just, uh, y'know, some novelties ... that sort of ... thing ... I guess."

"Well, what have you gotten already?" I look at the items in his hands: some bondage videos, rubbing oil, two or three magazines. Not exactly bachelor-party material and the look on my face lets him know I know it.

"Oh, just some magazines, a coupla videos ..." he says as he tries to cover them. "But I'm, um, I'm thinking I should get some, y'know, some funny, gag-type things. Y'know? Isn't that the norm for bachelor parties?"

I nod and walk around from behind the counter, then make him squirm even more as I lead him through the store. "That stuff would be in this aisle. You got your standard issue blow-up dolls, strap-ons, etcetera ..." I look at him and he nods like he doesn't know what I'm talking about - the phony. "You know, if it's a bachelor party, my boss has some strippers you could hire ... if you're looking for that sort of thing."

He looks totally uncomfortable at this point and I begin to feel sympathy for him. I mean, it's not like he's committing a crime. He's just being hypocritical.

He's not even really being that. All he was trying to do with all that lecturing was protect his daughter from me. He didn't know me from Adam. He didn't know what my intentions were. He didn't know they'd end up as honorable as I feel they are at this point.

And like Holly said, none of us is a saint.

So I decide to let him off the hook. "But that's probably too much," I say, referring to getting the strippers, which I think he might have actually done to perpetuate the deception. "I'm sure it's just gonna be guys getting together, having a few drinks, that kind of thing. You just want some stuff to, uh, give it some color."

Mr. Kinney nods.

"I'd say what you have is enough, then." I lead him back to the counter.

I feel bad that he's buying some items he wouldn't have, had he not felt the need to lie to me, so I ring up the items and give him my employee discount. It's only twenty percent, but he seems appreciative.

"Thanks, Brian," he says as he takes the shopping bag from the counter. "I appreciate your help."

"You're welcome."

We both know what's going on, but neither of us is going to draw attention to it.

"So ... I'll see you Saturday?" I say.

"Saturday?"

"The prom."

"Oh, right," he says. "You and ..." He looks afraid. "Um, you won't -"

"I won't say anything." I nod like a priest who just heard a confession - not that I know what that looks like in real life. I've seen it in movies, though.

He nods thank you and leaves.

Once he's gone, it doesn't take long for my brain to refocus on my dilemma regarding whether to tell Jennifer about Holly. But in a strange way, Mr. Kinney helped me make up my mind.

I decide I'm going to listen to my mother and say nothing. I'll just go forward and be a better boyfriend from now on. If Jennifer knew about Holly, it would only hurt her - as well as our relationship - just like it would probably change her relationship with her father to know he's been buying pornography and kinky sex toys for years. That fact probably wouldn't help her relationship with her mother, either.

So in this case at least, silence is golden - for everybody concerned. I just need to make sure she doesn't find out from someone else. But I'm sure Mike won't say anything. Why would he?

EIGHTH

All week I'm upbeat and relieved about my decision to keep quiet. On Friday night at the formalwear store, while I'm trying on the tuxedo for prom the following night, I mention to Jennifer that there's a kind of "prom eve" party tonight and ask her if she wants to go. "Or do you need to be home early?" I say.

"No," she says. "It's weird. My dad didn't say anything about curfew. Not even for tomorrow."

I smile wide, but she can't see it since I'm still in the dressing room and she's outside. "I guess he trusts me now," I say.

"I guess."

"So you wanna go tonight? Mike'll be there."

There's only silence from the other side.

"You there?"

"Yeah," she says.

"You want to go to the party?"

Again, a strange pause. "Do we have to?"

"No. I guess not …" I button up the tux and slip on the shoes, then take a few seconds to check myself out in the mirror. I look kind of older, handsome even, in the outfit. I strike an "International Man of Mystery" pose and laugh at my own silliness.

"How's it look?" Jennifer says.

"Good ... I guess."

"C'mon out. Let me see."

"No," I say to retain a little of the mystery, if not the international. "You didn't let me see your dress."

"But you're not *supposed* to see the dress beforehand."

I laugh. "I think that only applies to weddings."

"Wedding ... prom ... whatever."

So I exit the dressing room and try out my Man of Mystery pose for her. She seems to like it. I can even see a glint of sexual attraction in her eyes. I like that glint.

"I tell ya Mike got a limo?" I say, all suave.

She loses the smoky look. "He actually found a date?"

"Yeah. Some Archbishop Kennedy girl, I think."

"Figures," she says with a smirk. "Nobody at North Penn'd go."

"Why not?"

"Well, he doesn't exactly have the best reputation."

"I know he can be crude sometimes," I concede.

"He's more than just crude, Brian."

"What do you mean?"

"Well, he's always trying to, y'know, get girls to have sex with him."

I shrug, as if to chalk it up to human nature. Besides, who am I to talk?

"No, I mean, he does that to *everybody*," she adds.

"What do you mean? Like ... guys?"

"No. If that were the case I'd at least understand that he's overcompensating. But he's not. He's just ... disgusting."

"Oh." I laugh and shrug off her concerns. "Eh, he's all talk. Seriously. I've known him forever. Trust me. He's harmless."

"'Harmless'?" she says with an odd level of doubt. "I heard he practically tried to rape Tracy - on the first date!"

"Oh, c'mon. I don't believe that."

"I do."

"You know how people talk in high school. I think they just went to the movies or something."

She stares at me, unconvinced.

"If that happened," I say, "why didn't she press charges or something?"

"Brian. Grow up."

"What? I'm just saying. People make stuff up sometimes. Not that I'm saying *she* -"

Jennifer sighs and rolls her eyes in frustration.

"What?"

"Brian ... he even tried it with *me*."

"What?! ... No way."

She stares, deadly serious.

"When?" I ask with a doubtful squint I hadn't intended.

"Never mind. You don't believe me."

"I'm sorry. I'm a little ... surprised. That's all. Just tell me."

After a long pause, she says, "Okay ... but don't get mad."

"I won't."

"Well ... he's always saying things, first of all." I nod. Goes without saying. "Which, y'know, I can handle. But then ... well, you remember a while back when you had to go to work and he drove me home?"

"After the basketball game."

She nods. I wait for her to continue, but she doesn't - as if I'm supposed to know what she's talking about from just that.

"What?" I ask.

She takes a deep breath. "Well, he was kinda drunk, so I -"

"He was drunk?!" She nods. "I didn't think he -"

"Trust me, Brian. He was drinking."

"I'm so sorry. If I'd known -"

"I didn't even realize it until we got in the car."

"Jeez," I say. "I feel terrible."

"It's okay. It doesn't matter."

"It does to me. You know that, right?"

She nods. "So, anyway, I did what you do; I took the keys and drove."

"Oh, well, that's good."

She nods again. "At one point he told me to pull over and I thought he was going to be sick or something, so I did. Then he starts going on about how I can do better - meaning him, I guess - and how he sees how I look at him - which I definitely *don't* - and he knows I ... y'know, with you and, well, next thing I know he's *kissing me* ... or trying to. I mean, he did a little at first ..."

I find all this hard to believe and have unwittingly taken a stand of neutrality. This is, after all, my best friend we're talking about. "And what'd you do?" I ask.

"I don't know what he's capable of," she says. "So I, y'know, kinda played along ..."

The thought that maybe she's covering some kind of tracks crosses my mind. I'm ashamed for thinking it, but can't help it. I'm a guy. We have our doubts, our jealousies ... our insecurities. "What do you mean 'played along'?"

"I don't know," she says and gets emotional. "He was

kind of pushing on me and ... I was just so surprised ... well, not surprised ... but ... shocked that he'd actually ..." She lets the sentence trail off.

I nod for her to continue.

"So ... I basically told him what he wanted to hear ... y'know, 'Yeah, you're right, Mike, blah, blah, blah,' until he eased up and I could push him off me. Then I got out of the car. He tried to get me to come back in, but there was no way I was gonna do that."

I'm still listening, but not sure how to compute all this. It's too much info at once and my brain's overloaded with a whole range of contradictory thoughts.

"So I don't want to be in a limousine with him," she adds as a period to her story, "... even if you're there."

But I don't really hear that last part clearly. I'm still busy trying to figure out what really happened, if anything. It's hard to believe that my best friend would do that to me. "Are you sure he - ?"

Jennifer's vulnerable look turns to anger.

"Yes, Brian. I'm sure! I know he's like a brother to you or something, so maybe you don't see him the way everybody else does, but he's not a harmless little kid anymore. He's a pig."

She certainly seems genuine. And I have no reason to doubt her, except maybe for the fact that she's only telling me this now. "Why didn't you tell me any of this?!" I ask.

Her anger turns to outrage. "What's that supposed to mean?"

"Nothing. You just shoulda told me."

"And what would you have done? It's my word against his. You've known him all your life."

"Yeah," I say, then soften as I consider her and the time we've spent together and what she's meant to me and what I want her to continue to mean to me. "But you're my ..." I'm not sure what to call her. It's more than just "girlfriend." "You're ..." All I can come up with is, "You." But in that word I put everything that she is to me - and she knows what I mean.

She half-smiles warmly, moves closer, and hugs me.

As I pause to enjoy the intimacy, I play back eighteen years worth of instances in which Mike has behaved in ways that, had I not been his oldest friend and been blinded by my loyalty, I would have seen him for what he is. Without my built-in trust, I'd probably have no trust at all for him. But I don't know.

However, my rage at this particular betrayal, which, sad to say, I believe more as I think about Mike and what he's capable of, creates a tidal wave of emotion that smothers the intimacy with Jennifer - for the moment, at least.

I can't stand there and hold her lovingly with all this going on in me. I need to do something. And that something - the only thing, really - is to confront Mike.

I separate from Jennifer and peel off the tuxedo.

"What are you doing?" she asks.

"I got a party to go to," is all I can say.

I pack up the tuxedo and usher Jennifer to my car so I can go find Mike.

I'm a man possessed as I drive to the party where Mike said he'd be, march inside with Jennifer behind me, and prowl the house in search of Mike. Within seconds I see him. He's talking to some other kids in the corner of the kitchen and chain-sipping from a large plastic cup.

Now I'm not much of a fighter. In fact, I've never been in a fight in my life. I've never really felt the need. Or maybe I've never been angry enough.

However, this night I'm angry enough - despite the fact that it's my supposed best friend I want to fight.

Jennifer can see it and tugs at my arm to slow me down. "Brian. Stop. Don't," she says as I march right up to Mike and grab him by the collar.

"Hey, hey," he says in reaction to the stranger who's grabbing him. When he turns and sees me, it's obvious he's drunk and can't read my mood. "Hey! Yo, Bro. What's up?" he says. Then I guess it registers. "What're you - ?"

"You fucking hit on my girlfriend?!"

"What? What're you talking about?"

"In the car, the night you were supposed to drive her home ..."

Mike stares at me for a few seconds, then looks at Jennifer. He must realize Jennifer's told me the story and that I believe her. He tries to turn the tide back in his favor by making a face and saying, "Dude, she came on to *me.*"

I stop and think about the things he'd said about her and Rick. It reignites the old doubts I thought had been extinguished.

"She's not as innocent as you think," he says, then adds, as if he's read my mind, "Just ask Rick Schmidt. He's around here somewhere."

Weakened by doubt again, I loosen my grip on him. I look at Jennifer a second, then back at Mike. I'm not sure what to believe.

"C'mon, Bro," he says. "It's *me.*"

I look at Jennifer, who rolls her eyes.

"Who you gonna believe?" Mike says.

I hold my stare on Jennifer. Her disgust at Mike turns into pleas for trust from me as Mike continues to present his case.

"You weren't there. You didn't see."

I'm still in doubt ... until I realize the full impact of Mike's words. I smile slightly with relief at Jennifer and I think she can sense at that instant that I *completely* believe her.

She has no way of knowing Mike's defense is exactly what his father told me to say after the episode with Holly: "Rule Number One: Nobody sees you, you didn't do it."

And if I have my way, Jennifer will never know about that.

But now that I'm one hundred percent convinced of the truth regarding Mike, I can no longer contain my anger at him for what he's done to me - both now and through the years. All the digs. All the belittling. All that condescension. All the attempts to build himself up while knocking me down. All the things that so-called friends do to - and accept from - one another because they don't see the harm. It all comes at me with a fury.

I turn back to Mike and, without realizing it, raise my fist to hit him.

But something stops me.

It's Mike's face. All I can see is him as a kid. I see the boy in the Little League uniform ... who thinks it's his fault his parents are getting divorced ... whose mother's more involved in keeping her house neat and stoking the anger she has at her ex-husband than she is in giving her son her attention ... whose dad doesn't seem to have a lot of faith in him. I just can't hit him.

Then I briefly see him kissing Jennifer and raise my fist again.

But then I see the two of us as children, playing, thick as thieves. For all that he's done to me, still, he was *there* … and that counts for something.

So I can't be angry. I can only feel betrayed. And it saddens me.

"Jesus Christ, Mike. You're like my, my brother. And you go and …" I release my grip on his collar. "I would *never* do that to you," I say. "Never."

"Bro," he says, continuing to try and make me believe. "C'mon. It wasn't me."

But it's too late. I shake my head with a combination of disgust and disappointment and turn to walk away.

It seems like everybody in the party's looking at Mike with the same level of judgment. Maybe they've known something all along that I didn't know. I guess friendship clouds your perception. A lot of things do.

But that's not the end of it.

"Oh, yeah," Mike says, "Because you're so perfect."

I know where he's going with this and continue to walk away without saying a thing. I'm the last person to defend myself against accusations. Mike's right; I'm far from perfect. But Jennifer doesn't need to know that.

"A lot more than you are," she says to Mike, as if spitting the words on him.

"Hah," he says, "I guess he didn't tell you about Holly, then."

I turn and stare at him. I hope he can read minds, because what I'm telling him is, *Look, this is over. You did what you did and I'm letting it go without a fight. So let's stop it right now.*

Jennifer looks at me and makes a face. "Holly? Who's that?"

"Nobody." I wave my hand at Mike like a magician making an object disappear. "He doesn't know what he's talking about."

I turn and glare at Mike so Jennifer can't see me and repeat the mental message about letting it go.

But it looks like he's not reading me. Either that or, more likely, he doesn't care. "Go ahead, tell her, Mr. Perfect," he says. "My dad's favorite. Hell, *everybody's* favorite. Everybody loves Brian. Everybody wants to be with Brian. Tell her about the night you spent with a porn star."

Jennifer has a questioning look and I can see the doubt rise on her face.

I'm not going to lie to her, though. That'll only make things worse. I'm a terrible liar, anyway.

"It wasn't like that," I say. "It wasn't anything, in fact. She was looking for a place to eat dinner … and I, I went with her … to show her. Her bodyguard was there the whole time. It was a, a business thing. It's not like anything happened."

"Really?" Mike says. "Show her the bite marks."

Okay, the hell with our history; now I'm furious at Mike. I'd probably feel like getting violent again, but am forced to table it for the time being. Right now I need to save my relationship with Jennifer. And to do this, I need to attack Mike's already questionable reliability, or, at the very least, play stupid.

"What the hell are you talking about?" I say.

"She bit him," Mike says to both Jennifer and the rest of the crowd now watching the scene. "I saw the marks on his stomach."

I continue to look like I don't know what he's talking about, all the while trying to remember whether the bruise marks are still visible on my skin. I know the ones on my face and neck have healed, but what about the harder ones on my stomach and my back?

I think they're gone. But again, I try to end the subject by shaking my head at Mike like he's crazy.

"Go ahead, lift up your shirt," he says.

"Yeah. Go ahead," Jennifer says.

By now everyone's watching. I have no other choice. So I smirk and shake my head at both of them, then lift my shirt. I look down to see if the marks are still there or not and to my good fortune, they're gone.

"There. See? Nothing."

But what I don't realize is that the mere fact that I *looked* is as telling as seeing the marks themselves. Because if I was absolutely certain there were no marks, I wouldn't have had to look. I would know.

But I didn't. I looked. Like a dummy.

Of course, this realization only comes after seeing the expression on Jennifer's face. She seems about to cry, but only shakes her head in disappointment and through quivering lips says, "You looked," before walking away.

I grab her arm to stop her. "Jennifer ..."

She turns and through her sadness bursts a flash of anger. "Let go of me!" She shakes my hand from her arm and runs off.

I want to go after her, but figure I should give her a second to cool off - like when she found me working at Adult World.

So I do.

And instead, I turn back to Mike, my so-called best friend. "What the fuck ... ? What're you ... what did I ever do to you? You hit on my girlfriend, now you -" I can't get the words out I'm so outraged at how quickly my whole life, or at least my social life, has disintegrated before my eyes.

"I tried to tell ya she's lying."

I can't believe he's still trying to convince me of this -

after what he just did to me! "Why would she lie?"

"I dunno. Why do you automatically believe her over me?"

"Because I know you," I say. "I heard what happened with Tracy."

As I turn to leave, he says, "Right … and you know *everything*. Pfft. You know nothing."

"What the hell's that supposed to mean?" I say.

A crooked grin forms on Mike's face. "You don't know the truth about *anything*. You don't know about me and Tracy. You don't know about Jenny and Rick. Hell, you don't even know about your mom and my dad."

I have no clue what he's talking about - and my face must show it.

"Yeah. That's right," Mike says. "*Your* mom and *my* dad. She *fucked* him - while he was married to my mom."

"You're drunk," I say.

"Why do you think my mom and dad got divorced?"

Now he's just bullshitting. "Stop," I say.

"It's true. He's got pictures."

The idea that perhaps he's telling the truth and that somewhere there are naked photos of my mother, taken by his father, runs through my mind. I shudder at the thought. "You're full of shit. My mom would never … not with your dad."

"What, you think she's too good for him?" Mike says, then smiles.

Before I can answer the question - in the affirmative, of course - he says, "Ask my dad. He'll tell you."

All I can think to say is, "Fuck you," and brush aside the whole notion with a sweep of my hand.

I've wasted too much time on Mike's bullshit already, when I should have been chasing after Jennifer.

I bolt through the house, searching for Jennifer, and see her in a corner of the dining room talking to Rick Schmidt. She looks angry and they seem to be getting ready to leave.

I want to go over and yell, "What the hell!"

Instead, I try a more passive approach.

Jennifer sees me coming and turns away.

"C'mon, Jennifer," I plead. "Talk to me. I -"

"There's nothing to talk about."

Rick's still standing nearby. I give him a look that even he, with his few inches and tens of pounds on me, knows to back away from.

I nod that it's a wise move on his part and turn to Jennifer again. "I need to tell you what happened."

"You cheated on me. That's all I need to know."

"I didn't know what you were doing." I look at Rick again. He can obviously read the weakness on my face because as I say, "You were mad at me. I thought you were with -" he steps forward. My rage returns, full-force. "This doesn't concern you, *Dick*," I say. "So why don't you just step off?"

He laughs. Maybe he's remembered that he's much bigger and stronger than I am.

But I don't care. I shove him away, hard.

He comes back, but before we can get into it, Jennifer steps between us.

We both freeze like little children told by their mother to settle down.

Jennifer nods that it's okay for Rick to let me talk to her and Rick steps back, though not without a warning stare at me.

"I'll be over here if you want that ride, Jenny," he says, which I must say almost gets me back into it with him.

But he's going away, so now I can talk to Jennifer - and that's all that matters.

"Look," I say to her, "that night I thought you were with *him*. I was -"

"So you figured it was okay to be with this ... porn star?"

"No. But, I, I was a little drunk and ... she came on to me. But nothing happened."

"Did you kiss her?"

"She, well, she kinda kissed me," I say, again like a dummy. I don't know why I didn't just say, "No." I guess because I'm a terrible liar. I add, "Sorta like with you and Mike," to shift the focus away from me, if only a little.

"Isn't that convenient?"

"That's not what I -"

Her face turns to stone. "I don't ever want to see you again."

"Oh, c'mon ... you don't mean -"

"I mean it." She walks away.

Of course I follow. "Jennifer, I'm sorry. I'm sorry, I'm sorry, I'm sorry ..." I look like a pathetic fool in front of all the partygoers. It's a Public Display of ... Abjection - but I don't care.

"That's not gonna work this time," she says.

"C'mon. I love you."

"I loved you, too - at least who I thought you were."

I stagger from the blow, but struggle to recover. "What can I do?"

"You can't do anything. It's ruined." She walks away to Rick and as they leave, he looks back at me with a victorious smile ... the dick.

I struggle to make myself believe that she never told

me the whole story about the two of them and that perhaps she was indeed with him the night I was with Holly. I want to believe anything that'll make this less painful, but nothing works.

I'm mortally wounded. There's nothing to save here.

The only reliable person left in my life at this point is my mother. When I go home, even she's not there for me. She must be out with Gary again.

As I fall onto my bed, I'm overwhelmed by loneliness. Lying there, broken, I can do nothing but replay the last two hours of my life and try to figure out what the hell happened and how I got here.

I keep coming back to what Mike said about what I don't know and all that stuff about my mom and his dad. I don't believe it and he certainly has given me a reason to doubt everything he's ever said, but the more I push it aside, the stronger it comes back.

I'm probably just obsessing over it to keep from thinking about the loss of Jennifer and the prom - *oh, the prom!* - tomorrow night.

But then again, who cares about the prom? It's Jennifer I care about. Sex, no sex, whatever. I don't care. I just don't want to feel like this anymore. Loneliness sucks.

I call Jennifer again. No answer. I don't want to consider what she might be doing with Rick Schmidt.

Damn, I wish my mom was home; maybe she'd know what to tell me to make me feel better.

I call Mr. Welch. I don't know why. But it doesn't matter; he doesn't answer, either.

I'm alone ... completely and utterly alone.

I contemplate the unthinkable for an instant, but shake it off as quickly as it appeared.

The only escape left for me is sleep, but my brain's too busy working to allow me to shut it off. I need to do something, anything, to distract it, but am unable.

I figure maybe a *petit mort* release might help me relax a little, but can't even generate enough energy to touch myself.

So all I can do is curl up in a fetal position and attempt to do what I usually do when I can't sleep: I imagine myself staring at a blank canvas. But the blankness keeps getting filled with painful images, so I force myself to sketch an imaginary image on it.

I fight the urge to draw Jennifer and instead settle on a simple, nondescript, pastoral scene - someplace calm that I can escape to. I then fill it out slowly with imaginary paint and, thankfully, mercifully, before the painting is finished, I'm asleep.

NINTH

The morning after my social life crumbled into a million pieces, I wake to the sound of my mother in her bedroom having sex - which is a sound I can't recommend enough that everyone avoid at all costs. Trust me; it's the last thing a child should hear a parent doing.

She probably thinks I'm out working like I usually am on Saturday mornings and isn't concerned about making noise. I suppose I could make noise to let her know I'm there, but that might make it even more awkward.

Instead, I try to drown out the sound by covering my ears with headphones, but it doesn't work.

Great. I can't even wallow in my shame and agony in the comfort of my own house now.

So I go to Adult World.

Tommy's at the counter, which is strange because Robby was supposed to take over the shift for me. I ask what happened, but Tommy shrugs like he usually does when he doesn't want to tell me something.

"Is Mr. Welch here?" I ask. His car's in the lot, but that's never a guarantee of anything with him.

Tommy tilts his head in the direction of the back room, so I go back. Mr. Welch is there counting and organizing money.

"Brian, my boy," he says. His enthusiasm is a welcome change and a comfort. I think, *Would someone who had sex with my mom be this cool to me?*

But I can't really answer that. After all, look at Gary.

"What are you doing here?" he says. "Thought tonight was the big night. The *prom.*"

"Called on account of rain," I say.

He stops counting the money and turns to me. "What happened?" He looks concerned and it's nice, but I don't feel like going into the story.

"Nothing. I'm just ... I'm not going."

He nods and thankfully doesn't pursue the subject, although I almost wish he would. I could use an adult's perspective on the situation with Jennifer and, just as importantly, the stuff about my mom. But before I can get to any of it, he says, "Well, you wanna go to a party instead?"

I'm not sure what he means, but I have an idea.

"I need somebody to collect some money - for some dancers."

"What happened to Robby?" I ask. "Doesn't he usually do that?"

"Had to let him go."

"Really? Why?"

"Let's just say we had a difference of opinion. He started to think he owned me, instead of the other way around." He smirks and shakes his head. "Heh ... Give a guy a job, a start ... pfft ..." He looks up at me. "So, whaddya say?"

"I don't know ... Isn't all that, uh, y'know, a little ... illegal?"

"Illegal? No. Whaddya think I - ? It's just dancing ... entertainment."

"Well, at Mike's -"

"Oh, that was different," he says as he finishes counting and puts the money in his safe. "It was for Mike."

I make a doubtful face. He turns, sees it, pauses, then holds up a video. "Think of it this way: this woman here - hell, your friend Holly - they get paid to have sex with guys on film, right? Is that illegal? Immoral?"

"Well -"

"No. So if it should just happen to occur at a party between two consenting adults, how's that any different? Because I'm not filming it? What's worse?"

I'm not sure what to say.

He puts down the video and closes the safe. "Besides, I can't control what a woman wants to do any more than anyone else. It's *her* choice, her body. I have nothing to do with that ... and neither will you. I just pay 'em to dance. That's it. So ... ?"

He waits for my answer and when I don't give it to him, he says, "You really think I'm gonna risk all I own by breaking the law? What do you think I am, some kind of pimp?"

"No, no. I didn't mean -"

He comes close to me. "All right, then. So whaddya say?"

I'm not exactly thinking straight at this point, but still, it sounds questionable.

Mr. Welch puts his arm on my shoulder. "There's nothing to be worried about. It's a simple transaction. All you gotta do is find a guy named Eddie, he'll pay you, you leave. That's it. Get in, get out. Anything happens, I got your back." He writes down an address on a slip of paper. "How's seventy-five sound? Cash. Easy."

"Well, I am out a hundred bucks for my tux ... then there's the prom tickets ..."

Mr. Welch smiles, gives me a look like I'm haggling - which I'm not; I'm just thinking out loud - and looks up at the sky. "Have I trained this boy well or not? All right, a hundred," he says. "I'll add it to your pay."

"Yeah, uh, about that: I haven't been paid in a coupla weeks ..."

"Yeah, cash flow's been a little tough this week," he says. "I'll have it for you Monday."

I nod and don't think about it anymore. I'm already on to the real reason I came here in the first place. "Can I ask you a question first?"

Mr. Welch lets out a heavy sigh, as if I'm taking up his valuable time. "What now?"

"Um," I say, "I know you've known my mom for a while, you being neighbors and all - before you moved away, that is. Did, um, you two ever, uh ..."

Mr. Welch looks at me and waits for more.

"Y'know ..."

"No, I don't know," he says. "What do you mean?"

"Did you ever ... date? Well, not just date, but ..."

"Oh, *that* 'y'know'," he says. I nod. "Who told you that?"

"Um, no one," I say. "I just, I don't know. Something made me think ... It doesn't matter. I just wanted to know."

"Now, Brian," he says and puts his arm around my shoulder again. "Would I do that to you?"

"I mean, I know it would have been a long time ago,

194

when I was just a kid, so it's not like it's a -"

"Brian, when you were little, I was married. What the hell kinda person do you think I am?"

I look around me, at the surroundings, and wonder.

"What kind of person do you think *your mother* is?"

Well, he's got a point there. "I'm sorry," I say. "I just, I didn't -"

Mr. Welch releases me. "It's okay. Look, your mom was a good friend - like your dad was before he died - so I can see how you could think that, but, y'know, kids imagine all kinds of weird things about their parents - even when they're not true."

I consider it. Another good point. And Mike probably thinks those things more than most.

Yeah, that's what it is, I figure.

"Okay?"

I smile and accept his answer.

He rubs my head and messes my hair. "Attaboy ..."

He then hands me the address of the party that night and just like that the issue is resolved.

Still, there's something about this whole Mom/Mr. Welch thing that sticks with me. I don't know why. But later, when I'm at home watching my mom eat dinner and flirt with Gary in front of me, I get the sense that maybe Mr. Welch wasn't telling me the whole story.

I can't fight the all-consuming need to ask the only other person who knows the truth. It won't be easy to bring it up, but I *know* my mom won't lie to me ... I hope.

Once I decide to talk to her about it, I can't wait. And

before we're finished eating, I ask Gary if he can give me a minute alone with my mother.

"What are you - ?" my mom says and looks at me, puzzled. "We're eating dinner."

I look at Gary and he can see how serious I am. "Please."

He stands. "I'll just, uh, go watch TV."

When he's gone, my mom looks at me, concerned. "What's wrong? Are you okay? You upset about the prom? I know you were looking forward -"

"I don't give a shit about the prom," I say. "Sorry. I mean, I don't care. Well, I do ... but ... whatever. I need to ask you a question."

She nods and waits for me to speak.

I finally get the nerve to start. "Did you -" But it's a false start. I step back into the blocks, get on my mark, and try again. This time I think a bluff might be the best way to go. I don't know why. "Mr. Welch said something ... something, um, about the two of you - that the two of you had a, uh, a thing, once."

"A 'thing'?"

"Well, he, he, uh, actually said it was a little, um, more ... than that."

She smiles and shakes her head. "Oh, he *did* ... ?"

I nod.

"Heh," she says. "Well, I guess that doesn't surprise me ..."

"So it's not true?" I am totally relieved. "Heh. I figured. You know how he -"

"No, it's true," she says.

I stare at her to see if she's telling the truth. I have no idea why she would lie about this, though, so it's clear that she's being honest.

"Wait ... you did?"

She nods.

I feel like I've been punched in the gut. It takes me a minute to get my wind back. "And the two of you ... y'know?"

She nods again. There's not a shred of dishonesty on her face.

It's as wicked a curveball as I can imagine - even worse than Mike hitting on Jennifer - thrown right at my head: to find out my mother has *done* Mr. Welch - of all people! I mean, he's been good to me and all, but still ...

My mom's nod is not just a beanball, though; it's a wrecking ball. And in one swipe, it destroys every illusion I have about her. I mean, I know she's not perfect - no one is, as I'm learning all too well - but ...

"Aw, gah," I say in shock as I choke on my own thoughts and words. "You didn't. Tell me you didn't ..."

She shrugs helplessly.

"You actually ... you, you fucked him? Mr. Welch? You fucked Mr. Welch. Oh, fuck ..."

"Stop using that word."

"What? Fuck?"

"Yes. I'm still your mother."

"Well, what word should I use? Bang? Boff? Hump? Pork? Fungo?"

"'Fungo'? What the hell is 'fungo'?"

"It's a word Mike uses," I say, still processing this.

"Sex, Brian. The word is 'sex'. Yes, I had *sex* with Mike ... Senior ... Mr. Welch to you. Any other questions?"

I turn away. "I don't think I wanna hear this."

"You asked."

"And I'm beginning to regret it."

"It's not exactly easy answering it, y'know," she says. "But that's life: tough questions and tough answers."

"You couldn't at least sugar-coat it a little?"

"Why? You're not a kid - as you're so quick to point out. At a certain point you gotta stop eating kids' cereal."

I pause and consider this. It's a pretty appropriate metaphor. Perfect, even. And I suppose in the end the truth is more nutritional. Shame it tastes like Brussels sprouts.

"So then why didn't you tell me?" I ask.

"What does it matter?"

"It matters because now I look like a fool. You knew I was working there. You basically, you lied to me."

"No. I just didn't tell you. Didn't we have this discussion before? You don't need to know everything, do you? If you'd have asked, I would have told you. In fact, I just did."

I replay in my head all the times I've spent with Mr. Welch, even the ones when I was a kid. They all look different to me in this new light. "Jesus! No wonder he was so nice to me. Probably still wants to get in your pants ..."

"Brian ..."

"Mike says he even has pictures of you."

"So?" she says.

"'So?'!" This is getting stranger and stranger.

"Yeah," she says. "There were lots of pictures taken, probably many of the two of us. Your dad had a camera, too."

"What?!" *It's worse than I thought! Now my dad was involved?!*

"He was a neighbor, a friend. We'd have parties, barbecues, whatever ... people took photographs."

"Wait, whaddayou mean?" I'm thinking this was some kind of crazy swinger neighborhood or something.

"What do *you* mean?" she says, then after a moment realizes. "What, you think there're naked pictures of me out there?!" She laughs hysterically.

When she calms down, she reassures me, "You don't need to worry about that. *Nobody's* shooting me in the all-together. I never even let your father do that. Not that he wanted to ..."

Then a much worse fear comes to my mind. One I can barely conceive of. "When did this happen, exactly? Were you with Dad at the time?"

"Why?"

"I just want to know," I say. I can't admit this fear.

Her eyes widen with shock and she laughs even harder. When she calms down this time she looks at me like the child I am at this instant and says, "No, Brian. I wasn't with your dad. He was gone by then. So, no ... Mr. Welch is not your father ..."

I shrink from embarrassment at my own stupidity. But with the way things are going, who the hell knows? And it would explain all the niceness ... and that thing he said on my birthday about me coming home from the hospital - like it meant something to him. Also, how Mike is kind of like a brother - to say nothing of all the times he called me "Bro" or his "Brother from another mother."

"You really thought that?!" she says.

"Well, I don't know!" I say.

I can see the hurt grow on her face now that all this has come out. What she must think I think of her! It ain't good at the moment, I have to say.

"I mean, what the hell ... I don't know why you would have even fucked - had sex with, whatever - him in the first place!"

She shrugs and seems to slip back in time in her mind. "He wasn't always like he is now. He helped me out a lot back then. Your dad didn't leave us much."

"So, so ... what ... you did it for money?"

The look of offense rises back on her face. "What do you think I am?"

"I don't know!" My tone says it all. She could've done just about anything, I've lost so much faith in who she is, who I thought she was.

She looks like she wants to cry, but instead laughs in a weird way. The two expressions of emotion aren't all that different sometimes.

"He was still married to Mrs. Welch at the time ... wasn't he?" I say.

Her face straightens. She says nothing, but she doesn't need to. The answer's in her eyes, which, for the first time during the conversation, are not looking at me. They're aimed down at the linoleum floor.

"Jesus, Mom!" I say. It sucks feeling morally superior to adults at this age.

"I'm not proud of it," she says and looks back up at me, "but ..."

"But what?"

She tries to compose herself. "His marriage was bad. He'd already been with other ... not that that matters ... but ... I was ... I was lonely. I had nothing, nobody. I was on my knees."

The thought of what she might have been doing on her knees - to Mr. Welch - crosses my mind and I snort with disgust at it.

Any vulnerability that my mom showed is gone in a flash. She can definitely read my mind. "Don't you *dare* take that attitude with me! You think this hasn't been hard for me?"

"No," I say.

"You know, it's really easy for children to be judgmental. They haven't lived long enough to make mistakes. Hell, they've barely lived at all."

I nod in half-hearted agreement. "I just … I don't know … I guess I always saw you as … y'know … better than that …" This should be a compliment, but given the circumstances and the truth of it, the implication is that she's no good. And at this moment, I'm not sure how much or how little I believe it. I'm still in shock. I'm also angry that I should be so naïve, so unaware of my surroundings and the people in it.

Mike was right; I know nothing. I'm a child.

My mom looks like she has a dagger stuck in her heart - and I did the stabbing.

I turn away, ashamed at myself for saying what I thought.

Gary must have sensed something going on - he probably heard the whole thing, in fact - and now that there's silence, he probably figures he better check on us. He peeks his head in and says, "Everything okay in here?"

He's the last person I want to see right now. His presence only further sullies the image I have of my mother, especially given what I've witnessed - or heard, rather - them doing.

"Gary, this is none of your business," I say.

My mom shakes all the emotion from her face, as if wiping the past few minutes from her mind. "It's okay," she says. "You can come back now. We're finished."

"No, we're not," I say.

"Yes," she says and looks hard at me. "We are." She takes a breath and moves back to the table. "Go ahead. Sit. Both of you. Your dinner's getting cold."

Gary looks at her to make sure. She nods that it's okay. So he sits.

I, however, do not. "I'm not hungry anymore," I say and leave the house in a huff.

I get in my car and drive around town for a long time, trying to come to terms with the past twenty-four hours and the radical shift in my entire perspective that has taken place. I don't know how the hell I'm going to be able to go forward with all of it ... if I *can* go forward with all of it.

I've never been more alone in my life. I've never been more angry, more weak, more vulnerable, more betrayed, more ... well, you name it. I feel everything at this point. And all these notes are played in random succession, like a child pounding on a piano - or those people who were having sex on it in that video I saw my second day at Adult World. The horrific song it creates gives me a headache.

I need it to stop. I need to find a nice melody. I need something to make me feel good. The only thing that's left, the only thing I can think of, is Jennifer. She's still the best thing in my life, even if she doesn't want to be in it anymore. To me, she's still there, though - and probably always will be, in some small way.

So, with nowhere else to go, I drive to her house.

I park my car a few driveways down to make sure she can't see me coming. She probably wouldn't open the door if she knew it was me outside.

I stand across the street for a few minutes and get a read on the house. The light in her room is on - or at least it looks that way. It might only be light from the hallway spilling through her doorway.

Whatever, I think. *Home or not home. I gotta take a shot.*

At her door, after several failed attempts, I force

myself to ring the doorbell and soon hear footsteps approach. I don't think it's her, but pray that I'm wrong.

The door opens. It's Mr. Kinney.

So much for prayer. Even God has abandoned me at this point - not that I ever believed he was there in the first place ... or anywhere, for that matter. But that's a whole other issue ...

"Hi, Mr. Kinney," I say humbly, in case he's heard the story. "Is she here?"

"No," he says. "Since she wasn't going to the prom with you, she -"

That's right. The prom.

I wonder if she went, anyway. Maybe with Rick. He *is* a senior.

"Did she go with someone else?" I ask.

"No. Just went out with some friends."

I nearly collapse from relief and lean against the doorframe to steady myself. I want to cry.

Mr. Kinney bends down to get a better look at my face. "You okay?"

I shake my head and my face twists in pain. "I really screwed up, Mr. K. I don't know what to do. I said I'm sorry, I want to make it better, but ..." The emotion swells in my stomach like a wave of nausea. It's hard to hold down.

Mr. Kinney puts his hand on my shoulder. "Don't worry, Brian. I don't know exactly what happened, but believe me, at the end of the day, this isn't going to be as big a deal as you think it is right now."

I wish I could believe him, but I don't. "I don't know about that ..."

"Trust me. These things have a way of working out."

"Not this time, I don't think."

"You'll see. In the meantime, let me talk to Jennifer,"

he says.

I look up. It's as if God himself - if he existed - has shined a sliver of light down on me. I'm overflowing with gratitude.

"You'd do that?"

Mr. Kinney nods and for the first time I think he may actually like me. More than like me ... he cares about me. What mercy he shows!

I tell myself maybe he isn't such a hypocrite. Maybe he is a truly religious man. Maybe he has enough of the saint in him along with that little bit of sinner to be a whole person. Not that he's even sinned, really.

So he bought some adult material at a pornography store. So what? Doesn't mean he's broken any commandments or anything, does it?

No. Of course not.

"Oh, man," I say to him. "That would be ... that would be ... great. I mean, I know she respects you and if you could, y'know ... I'd really appreciate it."

"I can't guarantee anything," he says.

"No one can." And, boy, do I believe it at this point.

Mr. Kinney pats my shoulder and smiles.

The little hope he's given me is enough to keep me going forward.

It'll be okay ... I think.

"Go home," he says. "Get some sleep."

I nod, stumble to my car, and collapse in the driver's seat. I could go to sleep right then and there, but within seconds my phone rings. I grab it and look at the number.

Jennifer?

Nope.

It's Adult World. I know why whoever it is - probably Mr. Welch - is calling. The party ... the money collection. I'm late.

"Shit!"

I start the car and peel out down the street to do the job Mr. Welch is paying me to do.

As I turn onto the street where the party's supposed to be happening, I don't need to read the address Mr. Welch gave me to tell which house it is; people are going in and out of only one of them.

Because of all the cars, there's no street parking available and since I'm short on time, I pull as far in the driveway as I can and put my blinkers on.

I'm counting on this being a quick in and out. That's what Mr. Welch said it would be. Hopefully my lateness won't change that. Hell, hopefully my luck in the last twenty-four hours won't apply to *this*, too.

Inside, it looks like a fraternity party - or at least a movie version of a fraternity party; I've never seen one in person. Probably never will, either, where I'm going to school.

The party's loud and out of control. People are drinking and smoking and groping each other in corners and just generally indulging their lizard-brain vices as much as possible.

With all that's going on, and at such a loud volume, I'm surprised the cops haven't been called. But they probably will be, if they haven't already, so it's important that I get out of there fast.

"Hey," I say to one of the partiers, "Where can I find Eddie?"

He shrugs and walks away from me. I look around and think I recognize one of the guests, a guy I go to school with. He probably couldn't get a prom date. Or maybe the prom is over. I look at my watch.

Nope. Still another hour to go … like it matters.

The guy recognizes me and comes over. "Brian," he says. "Brian Hartman. How you doin'?"

"Fine," I say. I'd say his name back, but I forget it. I think it's Doug.

He starts to say something else, but before he can, I cut him off. "Hey, you seen Eddie?"

"Who's that?" Doug says.

"I don't know. I guess the guy throwing the party."

"Oh, yeah. I think I know who you're talking about. Try the basement."

"What?"

"The basement!" he yells over the loud music and points at the floor.

I nod thanks, then, after a quick survey, find the doorway to go downstairs. A man is in front of it like a Beefeater standing guard.

I reach past him for the doorknob, but he stops me.

"Twenty bucks," he says.

"What?"

"TWENTY BUCKS."

"What for?"

"You wanna go down, it's twenty bucks."

"The girls are down there?"

He looks at me like I'm an idiot. Of course they are.

"I was sent by their … employer … to collect money … for them," I say.

He stares at me a second and I stare back. I'm in no mood for games. He must see it, because he lets me go, but not before a "you better be" look.

I nod to reassure him and go down.

The finished basement resembles an old-style saloon. Besides containing a bar, there are beer and liquor signs all over the walls, a pool table, even a jukebox. Some poor father's playroom is being defiled by over a hundred college students - perhaps some high school students, too. I'm sure there are a bunch of average Joes there as well.

In the center of them all there are three dancers. Two of them I vaguely remember from Mike's party. Again, they're grinding away on all the horny guys, taking what money they can from them.

Surprisingly, some of the recipients are girls. It's kinda sexy and I stare for a minute or two until I catch one of the men grab at a dancer. She slaps his hand away and I get the feeling there's going to be trouble soon.

Oh, shit.

I figure I better get the money before things all go to hell, so I dart through the crowd yelling, "Eddie! Is Eddie here?!"

A partier points to a guy who at the moment is practically dry-humping one of the dancers. I move over to him and wait for him to finish, but since he doesn't look like he's going to anytime soon, I tap him on the shoulder. "Eddie?"

He waves me off.

"I'm Brian. Mr. Wel - Mike sent me. I need to collect for ... her ... them."

I look at the dancer, who smiles hello like she knows me, although we've never met. I nod and she goes back to focusing on Eddie, who points behind him with his thumb and says, "Rick'll take care of you."

"Who's Rick?" I say and turn around.

Eddie says, "My brother," at the same instant I see Rick Schmidt. He's dancing with another of the girls.

"Your name's Eddie Schmidt?" I ask to make sure we're talking about the right guy. I hope we're not.

But Eddie nods.

I hang my head. "Fuck." *What are the odds?*

I suppose I should be happy he's not out with Jennifer, but still ... like I need this now.

With a sigh I gather my strength and move to Rick. I step between him and the dancer he's with.

"Hartman?" he says with a smirk. "Dude, wait your turn."

"I need the money for her," I say to stick to business, "... for them."

"In a minute."

I roll my eyes and look back at Eddie, who appears to be - unless I'm hallucinating - about to get a hand-job from the dancer, right there in the middle of the room. It's insane.

I turn back to Rick. "No," I say. "I need the money now."

I ease the dancer aside.

"What the fuck ... ?" Rick says and shoves me away.

I can feel my anger rise again and think I have it under control ... that is, until Rick says, "Dude, relax."

In a flash, all the anger I have for Rick, as well as all the rage I feel for everything that's going wrong in my life at the moment - the stress and worry about my future, my doubt, the uncertainty about the world, every lesson I've ever had to learn on my own, the struggles I've had to endure, the responsibility I've had to take on since my father died, all of it - gives way.

"You know what, *Dude*," I say. "Fuck you." And I punch him square in the jaw. It's a good punch, too.

Rick staggers back, trips over the dancer's leg, and falls to the ground in a heap.

I've never done anything like that in my life and - *Oh. My. God.* - does it feel good.

I stand over him to savor the act, but am immediately confronted by Eddie. Before I can react, he punches me in the face. To my surprise, I take it okay.

I think he only hit me more on the side of the head, and my skull's pretty thick - as evidenced by recent events - so I only stagger back a little.

I quickly return and take a swing at him. I miss, but just as he begins to gloat, the dancer, who I guess is defending me, her fellow employee of Mr. Welch, kicks Eddie square in the balls. She's wearing a sharp pump, too. He doubles over and his face looks kinda like that old photo of Lee Harvey Oswald, the one where he's getting shot. It's hysterical.

I have no time to laugh, though, because Rick is now up and back for more.

As I step back and cock my arm, I notice that it seems the one punch of mine has started an entire brawl around me. It's like one of those Wild West saloon fights you see in movies. People are throwing chairs and bottles at each other. It's out of control.

In the middle of the chaos, I give a few hits and take a few. I think I give more than I get, especially in Rick Schmidt's direction. He clearly has the size advantage, but everything's been easy for him in his life. For me it's been a struggle, so I've got fury on my side ... and it's all coming out and aimed in his direction.

At one point, I've pinned him on the ground and am swinging wildly. I don't hear anything going on around me anymore; I'm too focused on what I'm doing.

I punch away until someone pulls me off, then turn to

take a swing at whoever this referee is and thankfully don't connect. I say that because it's a cop. The party has been raided, like I thought it would be.

I can't hear the music anymore because there isn't any. The room is silent and calm. I was apparently the last fighter still going. I think even Rick knew what was happening. I might have heard him say as much, but just didn't give a damn.

I look around at the crowd and drop my shoulders in surrender. "Oh, fu ..."

I hear someone say, "He started it, Officer," right before the cop grabs me by the neck, ushers me out of the house, and stuffs me into the back of a cruiser.

After the release of all that tension in the fight, I'm in an oddly serene state as I get processed inside the police station. Either that or I'm numb from the shock. Or maybe the past twenty-four hours have been too much for me to process and my brain has shut down altogether.

I figure in this state I'm probably better off in a jail cell for now. Who knows what else is in store for me out there?

Also, there's something comforting about knowing you've hit rock bottom. I even manage to nap at one point.

It's only when I get my chance to make a phone call - I left my cell phone in my car - that I become anxious again. I almost want to tell the officer to forget about it. I have no idea whose number to dial, anyway.

I don't want to call my mom. Even after our go-round, I don't want her to see me like this. And I certainly can't call Mike or Jennifer.

I think about calling Jennifer's dad, but that's probably not a good idea, either.

The only person left for me to call is Mr. Welch. He knows a lot of people, so I figure he'll be able to get me out - hopefully in a way that keeps my mom from ever finding out about it.

I collapse in relief when he answers.

"Mr. Welch. It's Brian."

"What? Whatsamatter?" he says. He can no doubt hear the desperation in my voice.

"Um, things didn't go so well tonight."

"What do you mean?"

"Well, I'll tell you about it later. Right now, though, I'm in jail."

"Jail?!"

"Yeah. There was a problem with -"

I hear a click, then nothing. Only silence.

"Hello?" I say. No response.

At first I think there's a problem with the connection, but quickly realize that's not the case.

He hung up on me!

I stare at the phone in disbelief and after a few seconds of painful contemplation realize what I have to do. I convince the officer to let me make another call, then take a deep breath and call my mom.

She answers and after I tell her where I am, she of course runs to the station without a moment's hesitation. She doesn't ask what's the matter, how it happened, what I did, nothing. She just comes to get me.

Gary comes along with her, which is a good thing, it turns out, because he happens to know one of the officers who raided the party. They went to high school together or something.

So, as I sit quietly in a cell and reflect on all the curveballs life's thrown at me in the last few months - and how I was so blind that I saw none of them coming - Gary works it out with his officer friend Tim so I can be released. He even gets him to throw out the charge. But Gary owes Tim a night out to dinner. He and his wife with my mom and Gary. Something like that.

"Like it never happened," is the phrase Tim uses as he winks and shakes Gary's hand after I'm set free.

I nod a heartfelt thank you. Tim looks at me and shares a look of bemusement with Gary before he goes back to work.

Of course, my mom freaks when she sees the bruises on my face, but I assure her I'm fine and don't need to go to the hospital.

"You sure?"

"Yes," I say. "I'm good."

She stares at me a moment to be certain, then accepts my answer.

And that's the end of the ordeal - or the legal part of it, anyway.

It's amazing; within fifteen minutes of him showing up, Gary's got me walking out the front door of the police station. He must be better regarded around town than he is in my house - by me, anyway.

My mom now gazes at him with more adoration than I've ever seen her have for anyone before. She might have looked that way at my dad when he was alive, but I would have been way too young to see it - or even recognize it, I imagine.

It's quiet as we drive home in Gary's vintage Mustang and he walks us to the door.

"You coming in?" my mom asks him.

He looks at me, then my mom, and with a warm

smile, says, "That's okay. I'll, uh, see you tomorrow."

My mom accepts his answer graciously. "Thank you. Thank you *so* much."

Gary makes a face like what he did was no big deal and says, "Anything for you."

He gives my mom a soft kiss goodbye and walks away before I get a chance to say thanks, too. I'm too choked by my shame to get it out, anyway.

My mom watches him the whole way as he gets into his car and drives off. She waves goodbye when he's at the corner and he returns it with a quick honk-honk of his horn before continuing on.

She's smiling. It's the kind of smile I've seen Jennifer have when looking at me.

I miss that smile.

Once Gary's gone, my mom and I enter the house.

We haven't said anything to each other in about fifteen minutes, so as we enter the kitchen I'm waiting for the "What the hell were you thinking?" the "Are you out of your mind?" the "Didn't I raise you better than this?"

But she doesn't say anything like that. After she takes a bag of snow peas from the freezer, places it on my cheek, and lifts my hand so I'll hold it in place, the first words out of her mouth are simply, "Are you hungry? Can I make you something?"

I shrug. I'm not hungry.

I sit at the kitchen table as she prepares a plate of leftovers, I guess for herself.

As I watch her go about her business and feel my face begin to go numb from the peas, for the first time in my life I see her frailty, her age. Not that she's old, mind you. It's not even really age, I guess. I think what I see is her humanity. I see all the years of struggle, all the scraping by to make ends meet, all the compromises she's had to make at work, at home, in her personal life, just to stay afloat and provide for me.

I feel horrible for having said, even suggested, what I did about her character. If anybody has strength of character, *had* to have strength of character, it's my mother.

"Mom ..." I say. The word kind of squeaks out of my mouth. She turns and looks at me. "I'm sorry about before."

She half-smiles and moves her head side to side in short bursts for me to say no more on the subject. "It's okay."

"No, really, I -"

"Brian," she says and holds the moment. "It's okay." She smiles and it seems the past twenty-four hours have melted away.

They are now pouring from my eyes in the form of tears.

Like I said in the beginning, we Hartmans don't usually show emotion. But you can only hold it in for so long, I suppose. Beats getting into fistfights out of nowhere, right?

"I don't know what I was thinking," I say through the waves of emotion. "I don't even know what the hell's going on."

"You're under a lot of stress. You're graduating in two weeks. You -"

"No. It's, it's more than that," I say. "I mean, I, I don't know who I am anymore. I'm working at this stupid job, I'm fighting ... getting arrested ... I actually called Mr.

Welch first tonight! I thought ... I mean, I grew up with him. You ... y'know ... I'm friends with Mike ... or I was ... and ... I, I thought he'd at least *care*."

She laughs as she puts the food in the microwave, then approaches me and rests her hand on my head. "The thing you gotta understand about a guy like Mike ... Senior - probably Junior, too - is, well, they're selfish. The rest of us are here to satisfy their needs."

She's right, I think. *Maybe that's what it all is.*

Am I selfish too? I wonder. *Have I been?*

"They're not like you or me," my mom says, as if answering my questions psychically. "They don't care about anybody else. They're like children that way ... scared little boys afraid to really connect to another person. That's why that business is perfect for people like Mike."

I nod in agreement, then wonder, aloud, "If you knew all that, why did you ... *see* him?"

"Well, of course I didn't know it at the time - same as you." The microwave beeps. The food's done.

"See," she says as she removes the plate. "Mike has always had a knack for making it look like he's the one doing the giving, like he's taking care of you." She sets the plate in front of me. "That is, until he has no use for you anymore."

I laugh. It's the truth.

She sits across from me and looks as though she's trying on a painful old shoe. "And, well, when you're lonely, like I was after your father died, you'll do what you need to for human contact, even if it's just a morsel."

She keeps the imaginary shoe on another second, then kicks it off and looks at me with a smile. "And believe me, he was just a morsel." She winks.

I laugh.

"Actually mentioned marrying me at one point," she adds. "You believe that?"

"Really? He did?"

She nods. "Can you imagine?"

We both seem to try, but the picture's impossible to paint.

"He would've loved nothing more than to own *me*," she says. "Heh. But I damn sure wasn't going to let him - or any man, for that matter - do that. So I told him it was over. Boy, you should have seen him ..."

"Got mad, huh?"

"Quite the opposite," she says with a sympathetic look. "Actually got pretty emotional."

"No! He cried?"

"Yup. Like a little-bitty baby."

I know she's probably exaggerating, but it's the funniest thing I've heard in a while and cracks me up. I can just see him getting all weepy.

Hah.

"It was pathetic," she adds with a laugh, then turns sympathetic again. "But it was nice to see there was at least a little bit of soul in there, though. I doubt there's much left."

I nod in agreement and watch as my mother seems to replay the last two decades in her mind. I can see in her eyes the pain of the death of my father, the struggle, the ups and downs, all of it - even the good stuff.

She's gone through a lot and seems to have grown for the experience. She's clearly wiser than I ever thought she was and probably isn't even aware of just how special she is.

I stare at her with admiration.

It seems to make her uncomfortable, though. She still wears the armor she always felt she needed to survive and doesn't do PDA's very well. But she seems to be getting better, perhaps thanks to Gary.

I'm working on that, myself - for both of us.

"I love you, Mom."

She stares at me and seems about to cry, but shakes it and points at the plate of food in front of me. "Go 'head. Eat."

I smile at her for another long moment and do as I'm told.

I look up once more to see a warm smile form on her lips as she watches me eat.

It's nice.

The next day I go to Adult World, first thing. Tommy and Mr. Welch are there. They're talking casually about something, but I don't know what it is. There's too much on my mind to pay attention.

"Oh, yeah, I'm gonna get the money," is the only thing I hear Mr. Welch say before I interrupt him by handing over my staff shirts and phone.

"What's this?" he has the nerve to ask. He doesn't even notice the bruises on my face. Either that or he isn't concerned enough to ask me about it.

"I'm quitting." I say it without a hint of hesitation. And I'm proud of myself for it.

"Whatsamatter?"

"'Whatsamatter'?" I say. "Look at me. I got into a fight trying to get *your* money. And when I called you last night - from jail - you hung up on me!"

Tommy looks shocked. He turns to Mr. Welch as if to see if this is true.

"C'mon," Mr. Welch says. "What was I supposed to do?"

"Help me out," I say. "That's what. I had to call my mom! You remember my mom ..."

"Ehh," Mr. Welch says as he swats an invisible fly in the air, "I knew you weren't going to get in any real trouble."

"Yeah, no thanks to you."

Mr. Welch looks at me and apparently tries to appear remorseful. It doesn't quite work on his face. "Tell you what: I'll make it up to you. Another dollar an hour."

"It's not about the money," I say.

"It's always about the money."

I can only laugh at him. If he was right, life would probably be a lot simpler - but not nearly as rich, I would imagine.

Ellis comes out from the booth area. He obviously senses something going on, because he has his headphones off to listen.

"You really want to burn this bridge?" Mr. Welch says. "With school coming up?"

For a lightning flash I have my doubts, but am determined to hold steady. I'll find another job, another way ... somehow. Working here is not worth the price.

This is driven home more as I look at Tommy. He nods, as if to show me that I'm doing the right thing. *Get out while you still can*, the look says.

I hope Tommy quits soon, too, so he can meet someone like the redheaded woman who was with her vibrator-buying brunette friend. Maybe he's already met one like her somewhere, but his brain is so warped from living like this, the way so many men - and women, too, I suppose - do, that he didn't know how to connect with her on any other level. And sex alone can only take you so far, I would imagine.

I look back at Mr. Welch and continue to hold my ground.

He looks offended. "After all I've done for you? I treat you like a son and this is the way you return it?"

"A son?" I ask with a laugh. "Well ... I guess that explains Mike."

"What's that supposed to mean?"

I don't want to get into it with him. It's over; no sense in dwelling on it. I just want to move forward.

"Nothing," I say and hand him a piece of paper with the total hours I've worked since he last paid me. It also shows how much he owes me - including the hundred bucks from last night.

I don't include the thousand-dollar "bonus" he talked about when he hired me as weekend manager. I figure that was a bullshit promise, anyway, like the car hookup and the country club membership. I just want what I worked for. "If you'll just pay me what you owe me ..."

"Now you want me to *pay you*?"

"Yeah. I earned it."

"Well, considering last night I probably lost more than I owe you, how 'bout we call it even? Consider it a life lesson."

"I've had enough life lessons already, thank you," I say.

He can no doubt see that the tough stand isn't working, so he softens, moves closer, and puts his hand on my shoulder. "Brian, my boy ..."

I'll admit it's a move that's gotten me many times before. But not this time. And not anymore. At least not from him.

"I'm not your boy!" I say and throw his arm off me. "I'm not your anything. I just want what I'm owed."

Mr. Welch stands there, looking powerless - I guess unsure what to do with me. He turns to Tommy and Ellis, who both stare back at him judgmentally. I can tell he's determined to win at least one battle and he comes back at me with, "How about this: You help me out today and I'll pay you when you're done."

I get the feeling at this point he's not going to pay me at all and that he might change his mind if I sucked it up for one more day. And he just said he would in front of Tommy and Ellis, so he has to go through with it. Plus, I earned that money. So I want it.

Still, I don't want anything more to do with him or this place.

"It's a lot of money," Mr. Welch says.

He's right; it is a lot. I'm still considering whether to give in when Tommy steps forward to save me. "Oh, for fuck's sake, Mike," he says. It might be the first time I've ever heard him call Mr. Welch anything other than "Boss." "Just pay him."

Mr. Welch seems shocked at the mutiny. "You stay out of this. This is none of your business."

"I thought I was the manager," Tommy says.

"You want to *stay* manager?" Mr. Welch says.

"You gonna pay him?" Tommy stares at Mr. Welch and waits for an answer.

Mr. Welch notices Ellis, who has joined in and seems to have taken my side with Tommy. I'm not sure if it's because they like me so much, or don't like Mr. Welch and have had enough of his crap. He's no doubt treated them the same way at times and maybe they're fed up. I hope it's a combination of both factors.

"Awright, awright," Mr. Welch says. "Go ahead, Brian, quit. I thought maybe you wised up, grew a sack, but I guess I was wrong."

He goes to the register and counts out the amount I wrote on the paper. I count it along with him to make sure he doesn't short-change me. I wouldn't put it past him at this point.

He starts to hand me the money, then stops. "You sure about these numbers?"

"Absolutely."

"I'm gonna check it on your timecard."

"You do that," I say and take the money from him.

I count it again, in front of him, to make sure it's correct - and more importantly, to reinforce my low opinion of him.

When I'm done counting, he smirks and says, "Happy?"

"Yes," I say and put the money in my pocket. I then nod a combination of thanks and goodbye to both Tommy and Ellis and turn to leave.

As I walk away, Mr. Welch tries to get one final jab in by saying, "Tell your mommy I said 'Hi'."

I freeze and debate coming back at him for his comment, but decide I don't want to dignify it with a response.

I never quite understood what that saying meant until this moment. The issue isn't so much about dignifying the comment, as it is about *un*-dignifying myself - and my mom - by responding to it and stooping to his level.

My only response is to shake my head and laugh as I open the door to leave.

Behind me I hear Mr. Welch say, "Who do I have to take his place?" to Tommy, but he gets no response.

Even without looking, I can sense Tommy's disdain for his boss, who still doesn't seem to get it.

"What?" is the last thing I hear Mr. Welch say before the door closes behind me.

EXTRA

Two weeks after I quit Adult World, I'm officially a high school graduate - cap, gown, diploma, and all. In the meantime, I've gotten a pretty good aid package from the University of the Arts, paid my deposit, and visited the school once more.

Now that the bruises on my face have healed - and the ones on my soul getting there - I've resolved to do nothing but look forward from this moment on.

It feels good.

I still haven't talked to Jennifer since the night before the prom, though, and in school she's done a great job of avoiding me in the hallways, which kind of sucks. I really wanted to continue seeing her - and not just to get to home base ... although that would have been nice.

So much for my birthday wishes ...

The whole thing saddens me more than I'd like to admit, but I figure if her own dad can't convince her to talk to me, then there's not a whole hell of a lot I can do about it.

It's like that saying everybody writes in yearbooks, "If

you love something, set it free. If it comes back to you, it's yours. If it doesn't, it never was in the first place." Yeah, it's corny, but true.

After the graduation ceremony, my mother throws me a party to celebrate. My grandparents are there, my uncle, cousins, our neighbors, friends, everybody who's been close to us - all except Mike, of course. She's cooked a lot of food for the occasion and makes sure everyone eats more than you'd think their stomachs could hold.

It's a nice gathering and with all the support and kudos - not to mention gifts - I get from everybody, I realize that perhaps I'm not as alone in the world as I thought I was. And not everybody is a selfish and deceitful person.

In fact, there've been a lot of people in my life that have had my back - and I was too pre-occupied with all the adolescent crap that comes with high school to realize it. I even learn that for the past few months Gary has been one of these people.

At one point during the party, Gary's friend Jeff, the one I bought the car from, walks over to me and says, "Hey, Brian. How's the car running?"

"Great," I say.

"You treat her right, she'll run forever," he says with a drunken slur. He then adds, "Best two thousand bucks you'll ever spend."

"Two thousand?" I say. I only paid him five hundred - what he was asking - and I remind him of that.

"Yeah," he says, "Right. And Gary covered the diff -" He stops when he realizes what he's saying. "Oh, shit!" He looks around, probably to make sure Gary isn't nearby, then leans in close to me and says, "Look, don't say anything. All right?"

We both look at Gary, who's in the kitchen being lovingly fed a forkful of food by my mother.

"Seriously," Jeff adds. "He'd be totally pissed."

I nod and Jeff runs away as if he might let slip something else he shouldn't.

I watch my mother hand a new plate full of food to Gary and kiss him. She continues for another few moments, even, without regard for all the people standing around her. I've never seen her act like that before … and I don't think it's from the alcohol. She seems as happy as I've ever seen her.

My Uncle Steve enters the kitchen with an empty plate and she immediately stops kissing Gary and goes back to work. She takes the plate from my uncle and puts a new pile of food on it. As she does, Gary backs up, out of her way. He looks awkward, even shy, as he nods hello to my uncle. I've never seen Gary act like that, before … but maybe I haven't really been looking at him all this time.

My mother hands the plate back to my uncle and looks around to make sure everyone else is taken care of. They seem to be, so she pauses to catch her breath and notices me watching her. She smiles wide and I correct myself:

Now she looks happier than I've ever seen her look.

When I wake up the morning after my graduation, I go down to the kitchen and find Gary cleaning up the mess left from the party. I don't see my mother, though, and ask him if she's still in bed. I can hardly believe it when he says she is. It's so unlike her to sleep in.

"Y'know, you don't have to do that," I say.

"I know," he says. "But it'll mean a lot to your mom. She's done enough."

I nod in agreement and pitch in.

"What are you doing up, anyway?" he asks.

"Gotta go to work."

"Oh? You got a new job?"

"Sort of ..."

He nods and goes right back to cleaning. I know he's doing it, like he said, for my mother, but he also seems to get some kind of pleasure from it. I think he's truly glad for the opportunity to help her. It's a far cry from the moocher I've always seen him as.

I get the feeling he would do anything he could for my mother. Hell, he even expended a favor - a big favor - with the police. And that was just for her son.

"Gary, I never did thank you for your help," I say. "Y'know, with the police."

"Eh," he says, like it's no big deal, "I figured the last thing you need at your age is a record."

"Well, I know you went to bat for me ... and my mother, so ... thanks ... I owe you one."

"Nah. No you don't."

"Yes. I do."

Gary lets the subject drop and we clean in silence for another minute or two.

"Look Brian," he says as he stuffs and ties a trash bag closed, then stops and looks at me. "I know you don't like me ..."

"That's not true."

"Hey," he says, "I'm not sayin' I blame you. I'm the guy who's -"

"- having sex with my mother?"

Gary laughs. "I was going to say 'in love with your mother,' but okay ..."

"Yeah? You're in love with her?"

He nods and smiles, as if requesting my approval.

"Well, she loves you, too," I tell him, without showing

an ounce of disapproval over it.

"You think?"

I'm surprised by his doubt, then consider how hard it is to read my mother - even when you're her *son*. "Trust me," I say. "She may never *say* it, but she feeds you, takes care of you. She only does that for the people she loves."

Gary thinks about it and since it's coming from me, he's gotta figure it's the truth. He seems happy to know it.

He carries the bag of trash to the doorway to take it out, stops, sets it down, and looks back. There's obviously something else he wants to say, so I stop what I'm doing, too.

"Brian, I don't want you to think I'm pretending to be your dad or anything, 'cause I know you're too old for that ... but I want you to know that if you ever need anything, money for school, whatever, you can come to me."

"You don't have to do that," I say.

"I know," he says. "But it'll mean a lot to your mom." He picks up the bag again and adds, "It'll mean a lot to me, too," with a wink before going outside.

I'll probably never ask for his help, but it's good to know it's there, if only for my mother. In that way, he's already a big help to me. And I'm glad he's around - and will no doubt continue to be.

As I drive down the street and head to my first day back to work after leaving Adult World - I figured I deserved some time off after all that happened - I see Mike packing his car for Senior Week at the shore.

I haven't spoken to him since the night we had it out - and I hadn't intended to - but for some reason I feel particularly mature at the moment and part of being mature is having the ability to face awkward situations - or life in general. Right?

So I slow down by his car and roll down my window. When he looks up, I detect a note of regret on his face. Whether it's real or not I don't know - or care.

"Hey," I say, without any emotion.

"Hey."

"Headin' to the beach?"

"Yeah," he says, then, I guess as a gesture of apology, adds, "You're welcome to come down."

I nod a half-hearted thank you and say, "I'm gonna be kinda busy ..."

Mike accepts my answer without any fanfare. The look on his face is one I don't recognize. He seems about to say something else, but I've already put the car back in gear and say, "Well ... take it easy."

The opportunity for whatever he wanted to say now lost, he just responds, "Yeah. You too."

I nod, ease my foot on the gas pedal and drive on.

I don't make a big deal of my first day back at Truman's. I simply punch in and say hello to my former - and now once again current - coworkers as if I never left. No one comments on my return, which I'm happy about.

I wonder if Dave said something to them about it so they wouldn't bring it up. I wouldn't be surprised, especially after how cool he was when I asked him if I could come back. He didn't even ask what happened -

probably because he could see by my face that the answer wasn't a pretty one. He just asked me when I wanted to start. I told him after I graduate and that was the end of it.

So here I am, back to doing all the menial jobs I've done before - collecting carts, bagging groceries, working a register, all of it - feeling kind of like Gary cleaning the house and finding joy in the simplicity of work. It's easier for me to do now.

At one point, while I'm stacking lemons in the produce aisle, I look up to see none other than Charlie, the porn aficionado I hadn't seen in Adult World for two months - and who I presumed was dead or something. But there he is, thankfully, and looking better than ever. I think he may have lost a few pounds, which he needed to.

I wonder what happened to him, then notice that he's not alone. He's with a woman - and holding her hand. She's about his age and kind of pretty. Classy-looking, even.

I rest my elbow on the lemon crate and watch as he interacts with her in a way that's slightly awkward, but tender nonetheless.

Good for him, I think. He not only stopped going to Adult World, but he has a good reason to.

He must sense me watching, because he turns and sees me. At first he smiles with recognition, but the look quickly turns to fear. He probably figures if he says hello he'll be forced to introduce me to his girlfriend and explain how he knows me - which I'm sure he doesn't want to do. Or he'd have to lie about it. That wouldn't be good, either - no matter how much Mr. Welch thinks differently about it.

Screw Rule Number One, I think ... *all of them. There are no rules.*

I nod hello to Charlie in a way that lets him know not

to worry about saying hi to me and he returns it. The woman he's with doesn't see the exchange. She's off picking a honeydew melon.

I tilt my head toward her and bow slightly to show I'm impressed. Charlie nods thanks at the compliment before she holds a melon up to his face and asks his opinion. He smiles in agreement at her choice and she puts the honeydew in their cart.

He gives me one last grateful look as they walk on, hand in hand. It's kind of sweet to see him behave that way. For a moment I envy him and can't help thinking of Jennifer.

I miss her.

Even more than that, I miss *me* with her. I miss that more innocent, wonderful version of me that I seem to have lost over the past few months.

But no matter how much pain I feel over my loss, I can't feel any regret over the relationship itself. I'm not sure it's always better to have loved and lost than to have never loved at all, but in this case it is.

I may not have gone all the way - to home base, as they say - with Jennifer, but I got a whole lot more out of my time with her. In fact, at this point I can see that there's a hell of a lot more to human relationships than can possibly be described with baseball terms.

I decide that I need to tell all this to Jennifer. Maybe it'll help ease the pain and allow me to move on.

I know it's the end of an era for me. But with each end there's a beginning - and with each beginning there must be an end, I suppose. I'm not sure which is which ... and that's okay.

I guess part of growing up, life itself, even, is learning to not only see the world around you for what it is, but be willing to accept all the changes that come with it. In the end we don't have much choice, do we?

And if I'm going to be the kind of artist I want to be - or, hell, the kind of *person* I want to be - I need to keep my eyes and ears, and more importantly, my mind and heart, open to it all - the good and the bad, the sweet and the sour.

I put the last of the lemons out on the shelf and head toward the front door to call Jennifer from the payphone outside.

Dave sees me and says, "You're not leaving us again, are you?"

I laugh and say, "Nope. Just gotta make a call. I'll be right back."

He pats me on the shoulder and says, "Good man, Good man ..."

I walk on and notice the sticker on the automatic door as it opens for me. It reads, "One Way. Keep Going."

So I do.

Made in the USA
Lexington, KY
14 July 2012